CW00449985

CHRISTINA BAUER

First Published by Ink Monster, LLC in 2015
Ink Monster, LLC
34 Chandler Place Newton, MA 02464
www.inkmonster.net

ISBN 9780990635260

For Kim Stern

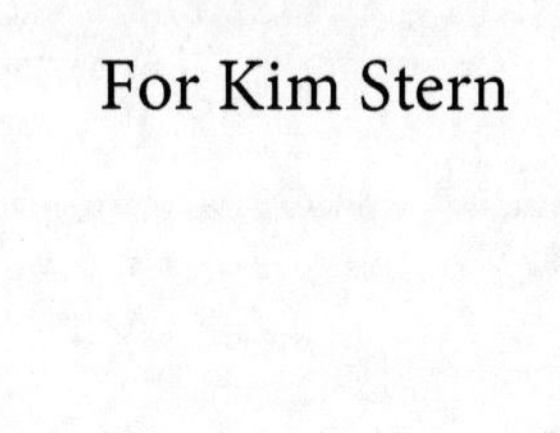

Chapter One

I am so late.

My heart beats at double speed while I rush down a marble staircase in the Ryder Mansion. If I were a doll, I'd be Action Librarian Barbie, The Super-Late And Extraordinarily Stressed-Out Edition. I glance at my watch and cringe. My lecture on *Magic Across The After-Realms* should've started twenty minutes ago.

The President of Purgatory waits for me at the bottom of the stairs. Her mouth presses into a thin frown.

"Portia, you're finally here," she says. "We were getting frantic."

The President's known for being tough on crime, corruption, and well, everything really. But she's also my grandmother. When it comes to family, Gram's a softie who worries like crazy.

"So sorry, Gram. I got caught up."

Her eyes widen with alarm. "It's your Firmament

spell, isn't it? You've been working on that non-stop."

The magical Firmament is what holds the after-realms together. Void demons have been attacking it for years. My spell will show the damage. Worst case scenario? All the after-realms could fall apart. Question is, will the catastrophe hit in six months or six hundred years?

My stomach twists with dread. *My intuition tells me it's closer to six months.*

"When do you think you'll finish the spell?" asks Gram.

"Any day now."

"That's excellent news. We'll finally know if danger is imminent." Her face beams with pride. "My brilliant grandbaby. After all the years of hard work, you must be thrilled."

I try to muster up a smile; I can't.

"Something else is wrong," says Gram. "What is it?"

I try to play it cool, but I can't stop the splotches of red that appear on my cheeks. "I was, uh, talking to someone before."

Gram lowers her voice to a hush. "Was it a boy?"

My heart sinks. *Technically, it was a boy. In reality, it was a disaster.*

Trouble is, I should be a man killer. I have all the ingredients. I'm nineteen years old, not terrible to look at, and a princess to boot. Plus, I'm part Furor dragon, which means that I should have supernatural powers over lust and wrath. But I'm the opposite of a man killer. More of a man frightener.

Gram's features soften with concern. "Please tell me what happened, honey." It's the 'honey' that gets me, every time. "Did you really talk to a boy?"

"Maybe."

"Oh, Portia!"

"Please try not to make it a thing. It didn't go well."

Gram stares at me expectantly. Her face is so open and understanding, I can't help but spill my guts. "I've been having flirty conversations with this guy, Alex, who works at the dry cleaner. But it was all by phone, you know? He never saw me. And I never wrote my real name on any of the slips, so he didn't know I was…"

"High Princess of the thrax and the granddaughter of the President of Purgatory?"

"Yeah, that." I anxiously shift my weight from foot to foot. "Anyway, today I needed to pick up my suit for the lecture. So, I decided to go in person." Alex looked adorable through the store window. He had blond hair, tawny brown eyes, and a sweet lion's tail. "Once he saw me, he freaked out and ran away." I spent an hour moping on the couch. Not my best morning.

On reflex, I brush my fingertips across the black tribal markings near my right eye. These are why Alex panicked. My marks frighten everyone. I've had them since birth. There's no hiding them. No removing them. And no avoiding what they mean. One day, I'll transform into one of the Void. A weight of sadness settles into my bones. "I should have expected it."

Gram gently guides my hand away from my eye. "Someone cast that spell on you, am I right?"

I nod.

"Then, there must be a way to break it. We'll

never give up." She lifts her chin defiantly. "And you're a marvel. Only nineteen years old, and look how much you've learned about magic. There's a way to break this thing and you'll find it."

I try to force another smile. It doesn't happen. Normally, Gram's pep talks work like a charm. But I'm not feeling it today. "You know me. I'll get my head together. Alex threw me off, that's all."

"Oh, honey. I may be old as dirt, but I remember talking to boys. How you look? It can *feel* very important when you're young. That's all an illusion." Gram sets her fist over her heart. "It's what's inside that counts."

Here it comes. No one gives a better 'be yourself' lecture than Gram. Most days, it works great. But today, all I can picture is the terror on Alex's face. Sure, we'd totally connected on the phone, but did that make any difference once he saw I was Marked? Not at all. "Gram, I wish people saw what's inside. I really do."

"Listen to me carefully, Portia. I'm a quasi-demon. Your grandfather's an archangel. According to our DNA, we should be enemies. But when I look at him, I don't see an archangel. I see Xavier. That's love, and that's what you need. I'm not saying it'll be easy, honey. I'm saying that you're worth it."

Gram takes my hands. Though her fingers are slim and dainty, her touch is firm as steel. "As a matter of fact, nothing worthwhile is easy." She gives my hands an encouraging squeeze. "But I know my grandbaby. You're a fighter."

I offer her a sad smile. "I can barely hold a dagger."

"That's not what I mean and you know it." She steps away and releases my hands. "Now, be honest with me. If you're too upset for today's lecture, you can cancel."

I stare at the closed door. If I walk out now, I know where that path leads. More hiding out in my penthouse, reading books, and practicing spells. *Alone*. I straighten my shoulders. Some risks are worth taking. "All right, Gram. Let's go."

"Now, that's my girl."

Gram and I walk down the hallway and into the packed ballroom. My body goes on high alert. Everything seems to warp and lengthen, like I'm looking through a fun house mirror. The tall French doors seem to tower impossibly high. The crowd's chatter echoes in odd ways. And all the faces somehow multiply by the second. I wipe my sweaty palms on my tweed skirt.

Why did I agree to this again?

If the full room makes Gram nervous, she doesn't show it. With an effortless grace, Gram steps up to the podium and speaks into the microphone. The crowd instantly quiets.

"Good afternoon, everyone. Welcome to our monthly lecture series for diplomats…"

As Gram does her introductory stuff, I scan the space and try to dampen my rising panic. The audience includes representatives from all five lands of the after-realms. There are angels from Heaven, quasi-demons from Purgatory, and ghouls from the Dark Lands. There are even a few full-blooded demons here, although they're all flanked by guards. And finally, there are a handful of demon-fighting thrax from Antrum. That's my father's side of the family.

"And now, it's my sincere joy to introduce our guest speaker." Gram gestures to the few thrax in the room. "Some of you already know her as Princess Portia, heir to the throne of Antrum. But I see a different side of this young woman. My granddaughter is one of the foremost experts on the different types of magic used across the after-realms."

Gram shoots me a proud glance. I inwardly cringe. No question what's coming next—Gram loves to talk about how smart I am. It's not my favorite topic.

"Portia has been named to the Angelic Council for Academic Excellence," says Gram. "She tested out of the human equivalent of high school and college at the age of thirteen. She was also awarded the Golden Pentagram for achievement in witchcraft. Portia is the only spell caster known to have mastered all forms of Level One magic."

Gram leans in to the microphone, her brown eyes glittering with delight. She's on a roll now. "You know, this reminds me of a story."

Reminds her of a story? Kill me now.

"My granddaughter's nineteenth birthday was just last month. Portia always makes a big book donation in honor of her birthday, and you know what? My granddaughter has given more than five thousand books on magic to Purgatory's libraries. Many of them are rare editions."

Gram shoots me a friendly half-wave. I try to grin back, but it might look like I have gas pains. The more Gram talks, the more I want to kick off my heels and run for the hills. I don't do attention. Period.

Before I can make any real escape plans, Gram ushers me to my place at the podium. "Therefore, without further ado, I present the Princess Portia."

Gram bows slightly and steps away. My heart thumps so hard, I feel the beat in my throat. I stare blankly into the crowd.

You can do this, Portia. You've been practicing your speech for ages.

"Canopic jars," I say in a full voice. "Does anyone know how they work?"

Evidently no one knows, as the room stays deadly quiet. My skin prickles with anxiety. This is not going well.

Thankfully, all my rehearsing pays off. My mouth starts moving on its own, following the familiar course of my presentation.

"Canopic jars were used by humans in ancient Egypt. We use them in the after-realms, too." I lower my voice to a conspiratorial whisper. "Only unlike humans, we don't fill the jars with body parts."

A few chuckles echo through the crowd. My confidence rises. "Canopic jars are best used as a supernatural batteries. Energy goes in and gets doled out slowly over time. The Firmament uses this principle, too." Some confused looks appear in the audience. I frown.

Oops, I may have lost them there.

"How many of you are familiar with how the Firmament works?"

A few people raise their hands. Most look even more confused. "The Firmament is an invisible magic network that holds the after-realms together. At the heart of this system, there are four Sacred Trees." I pick up the glass of water sitting atop my podium. "Think of this as a Sacred Tree. The water inside is Firmament magic. It slowly evaporates over time, feeding the roots and branches that connect all the after-realms."

I scan the audience. The confused looks have disappeared. My confidence soars. With that, I launch into a detailed explanation of the magical underpinnings of the after-realms. The more I talk, the easier it gets. After a while, it's hard to tell how much time's gone by. I don't really mind, though. Now, I'm the one who's on a roll.

I lean closer to the microphone. "There are four magical researchers who've done serious work on the Firmament. Two of these have theories I find useful."

Gram slips up to my side, her face all smiles. She gently nudges me away from the mic. "My, that does sound interesting. Sadly, I'm afraid we're nearly out of time."

My brows lift with surprise. "It's already been thirty minutes?"

"You've been up here for almost an hour, honey."

An hour? I can't believe it went by so quickly. The audience looks sleepy and dazed. My heart sinks. Maybe that last bit on magical researchers was too much. I turn to Gram and speak from side of my mouth. "What do I do next?"

"Perhaps you can take a few questions?" suggests Gram.

At these words, about a hundred hands zip up into the air at once. Gram gestures to a cute kid with a mop of ginger hair. "How about we start with this young gentleman?"

The boy bounces on his seat with excitement. He appears so sweet and harmless—all messy hair and freckles—that I take Gram's suggestion.

"How about you?" I point to the boy. "What's your question?"

The kid hops to his feet. "Where's your tail?" As he speaks, the boy twists his own lizard tail between his fingertips. "Did it get cut off or something?"

A jolt of anxiety hits my bloodstream. The fact that I don't have a tail really worries the general quasi population. "No, I was born without a tail."

Some members of the audience shift, uncomfortable in their seats. I can almost see their commentary hovering above their heads in cartoon-type thought bubbles. *Real quasis have tails, end of story.*

I worry my lower lip with my teeth. I need to lighten the mood here. I inspect the boy and guess why he asked the question in the first place. "But I bet I know someone who can lose their tail and regrow it."

The kid's eyes go big as saucers. "Yeah, I can."

At this point, the boy looks totally adorable. The crowd lights up with happy faces. Some photographers crouch-walk closer to the boy, all the better to get a good shot. Flash bulbs go off like fireworks. My heart lightens. At last, a front-page picture that won't make me cringe.

"Thank you, Princess," says the kid.

I smile from ear to ear. This is totally working. Without thinking, I gesture to the man who's next in line, his arm held high in the air.

"How about your question, Sir?"

The guy rises. "Roy Cotter, Purgatory Enquirer."

My heart sinks to my toes. This creep is one of those reporter-stalkers who follow me around looking for tabloid headlines. They always print the same stuff—how any second now, I'll turn into a demon, launch my secret plan, and overthrow Purgatory's government. Not that I blame the quasi population for being jumpy. We had a demonic diplomat who seemed harmless—that would be Armageddon—and he ended up leading a marauding army through Purgatory.

Roy stares at me eagerly, his dark eyes glittering with excitement. How could I have missed him? He's tall, bony, and has a scorpion's tail. Not easy to forget.

"When will you turn into a Void demon, Princess?"

Gram leans into the microphone. "You know our official stance on this topic. My granddaughter has had a spell cast on her. She has some unfortunate marks. That is all."

I press my lips together, hard. It's all I can do not to scream the truth into the microphone. I am Marked for the Void. And worse than that, those monsters are destroying the after-realms. It's only a question of when.

Maybe I can just say one little thing.

I raise my pointer finger. "Actually, when it comes to the Void—"

Gram grips my hand tightly, stopping me. A warning flashes in her brown eyes. I know that look. She doesn't want me talking about the Void and the Firmament. Not yet, anyway. We need to know if it's an imminent threat.

Roy glares at me, a challenge in his eyes. In the past, I've always agreed with Gram about holding off on the Void news until we had more specifics. But today, the truth bubbles up inside me, dying to get out.

"What do you say, Princess?" asks Roy. "Are you Marked for the Void or what?"

"I'm not here to disagree with the President," I say carefully.

"Ha! That's what we call a non-denial denial... Which means that you *do* think you'll turn into one of the Void. Come on, we all know it."

His words hit me like fists. *My tragedy is his next headline, nothing more.* My heart feels hollowed out and empty.

Gram sets her hand on my shoulder, gently pressing me away from the podium. "My granddaughter is not responding to that ridiculous accusation."

Normally, this is the part where I stiffen my spine, shut my mouth, and tough it out. That isn't happening this time around. Instead, something snaps inside me. There's almost an audible ping through my soul. Suddenly, I'm sick to death of concealing everything that I am. The guy wants an answer? He'll get one.

I lean into the mic. "No, I've got this."

"If you're sure, honey."

"Positive." Fresh rage corkscrews up my spine as I scan the audience. The anticipation turns so heavy, you could cut the air with a chainsaw. "Am I Marked to transform into a Void demon?" I drag out the moment for extra emphasis. "Absolutely."

A chorus of gasps fills the room. It's a satisfying sound.

"Perhaps we should end questions now," says Gram.

"With all due respect, Madame President," counters Roy. "The people of Purgatory have a right to know what's happening with your granddaughter, especially since you let her run wild." His mouth twists into a sneer. "We know what happens when a full-blooded demon goes free in Purgatory."

More anger spikes through my soul. "Worrying about full-blooded demons is a waste of time. The real threat goes beyond Purgatory."

The crowd gasps once more. Roy rocks happily on his heels. "Knew it! You're planning to conquer the after-realms. It's Armageddon all over again. This, my friends, is why full-blooded demons always have an armed guard."

Rage jolts through every muscle in my body. *How can he be so blind?* "You're focusing on the wrong thing!" I pound the lectern for emphasis. "I've researched this every way you can think of, and the fact that I'm Marked isn't what's important." The audience stares at me, dumbfounded. "This is a sign. Someone's warning us about the Void."

Worried chatter breaks out through the crowd. Roy's features brighten. He just got the scoop of a lifetime and he knows it. "Is that an official statement? You're turning into one of the Void and know about their plans to attack."

Rage seethes under my skin. "The Void are tearing apart the Firmament that holds the after-realms together," I say. "That's as official as it gets. Whether or not I'm one of them doesn't make any difference."

Gram wraps her arm around my shoulders. She's the picture of smooth. "For the record, my granddaughter is an expert on magic, not a representative of the government of Purgatory. If she has reason to believe that the Void are a threat, then I'm sure she has the documentation to support her claim. However, that does not mean that threat is immediate."

Roy starts to talk again, but Gram simply raises her hand and speaks in a deadly soft voice. "That's enough. I realize the quasi are wary of full-blooded demons. That's why I've supported the Senate's regulations on keeping them guarded within our borders. But to extend this scenario to my granddaughter is simply unacceptable." Her tone says that this is not up for discussion. "The lecture is over. We'll now retire to the gardens for more refreshments."

For the first time, I notice a series of servants standing by the French doors that line one wall of the ballroom. Acting in unison, they motion the crowd to step out into the gardens. The audience leaves so quickly, it's like a gunshot went off in the ballroom.

Gram pulls me aside and kisses my cheek. "That was a solid step forward, honey."

I lift my eyebrows in disbelief. "That was an all-out catastrophe, Gram."

"Give it time. Today, the quasi people saw that you're impassioned about their welfare. They didn't see a demon; they saw a young woman with a good heart."

Her words soothe my frazzled nerves. My anger cools, only to be replaced by a hot wave of embarrassment. "I'm so sorry I let loose on the Void. I know we agreed to keep it a secret."

"It's fine." Gram stiffens her spine. "More than fine, actually."

"What do you mean?"

"We're way past due to start messaging this to the general population. Xav's been on me about it for ages. I just wish we knew the timeline we're looking at."

"I'll finish the spell soon. I promise."

Gram sets her palm on my cheek. "You've such a good heart. Whoever cast that spell on you, they knew what they were doing." She runs her fingertips along my marks. "There's no one better to find out what's happening with the Firmament."

Warmth and pride seep through my chest. "Thanks, Gram."

"Why don't you take a break first? Xav told me that he found you some new magic books."

My eyes widen with excitement. "The medieval alchemy series?"

"That's the one." She gives me another quick peck on my cheek. "They're on the desk in his office."

"I'll stop by right away."

"Great idea." She makes shoo fingers at me. "Now, take the rest of the afternoon off. You deserve it."

Gram walks away while glad-handing everyone in sight. Turning on my heel, I beeline toward my grandfather's office in the Ryder mansion.

Alchemy books, here I come.

Chapter Two

I quickly find the office. It's the only one with a snarky poster on the door: a pic of a rainstorm with a caption that reads 'Purgatory, because sunshine is for losers.'

I knock lightly. "Hello Pops? Are you here?"

No response.

The door's unlocked so I walk right in. The place is decorated in all manly man stuff: leather club chairs, recessed lighting, and dark violet walls. There's even a wide balcony that makes it easier for him to land, angel-style.

I spot the alchemy books right away. The leather-bound volumes sit in a neat stack on his mahogany desk. I gently turn the old vellum pages and marvel at the illustrations. Reading a book is like coming home. Everything's warm and cozy. If only people could be that way.

Something rustles on the balcony. I set aside the

book to check things out. Peering through the balcony's glass doors, I find someone waiting outside: a muscular guy with black tousled hair. He wears jeans, biker boots, and a leather jacket. He's a total bad boy and a handsome one, too.

Wait, what?

I never go for the bad boy type. I like my men clean-shaven and buttoned up with nothing out of place. You know, the kind of guy who irons his jeans. Sure, those men look at me in horror, but at least they're usually polite about it. I consider that a win.

I frown. Chances are, this guy will react the same as all the others. I should walk away. There's a reason I'm nineteen and I've never had a full conversation with a man who's not a relative. I nod once to myself, the decision made. I am definitely leaving right now.

For some reason, I don't go anywhere.

Instead, I keep right on staring. The guy leans casually against the outer wall of the mansion, his right boot propped against the brick siding. His long, black tail sways lazily behind him. I give myself a mental kick in the butt.

You need to leave. *Go, go, go!*

I do no such thing.

Not only do I stay in place; I try for a better view. No matter how I shift, I can't see the guy's face. My skin tingles with curiosity.

Screw it. I'm going in.

Part of me knows that this is a big mistake, but I can't stop myself for some reason. With silent steps, I walk onto the balcony. Instantly, an electric awareness charges the air between us. The guy starts turning toward me, and then stops. Moving slightly, he refocuses his gaze on the line of trees. Rain patters on the tin canopy that stretches above our heads.

There's no question about it. I saw that half-look. This guy totally knows I'm here. Still, he doesn't turn to greet me. Instead, he stares off into the trees, his tousled black hair hanging over his eyes.

For a full minute, I look the guy over. He's well over six feet tall with broad shoulders that are more than twice as wide as mine. From the way he stands to the set of his jawline, every inch of him exudes confidence, power, and trouble.

"Hi." My voice comes out about an octave higher than normal.

Smooth, Portia.

The Mystery Man slowly turns to face me. At last, I get the close-up I've been craving. The man has intelligent brown eyes, a nose that's been broken a few times, and scar along his strong jawline. The imperfections only make him more appealing. He watches my stare and bit by bit, his full mouth arches into a crooked smile. Butterflies take up residence in my stomach.

"Hullo, luv." His accent is British, deep and hypnotic. Surprisingly, those words aren't accompanied by any signs of terror. It's dumbfounding. I stare at him for way too long without saying anything.

Start talking, Portia.

I revert to the basics. This is Pops' office, after all. "Is the Archangel Xavier expecting you?"

A mischievous light twinkles in his liquid-brown eyes. "Without a doubt. Are you here to keep me company while I wait?"

A jolt of happiness moves through me. He doesn't seem frightened of me, but maybe he hasn't noticed my marks yet. It's a little dark out here.

"Sure, I can stay with you, but…" I gesture around my eye and wince, waiting for the terrified look to cross his face. "That's only if you don't mind."

His smile doesn't waver. "That you're a Princess?"

"What?" I must have heard him wrong. "Did you say Princess?"

"That I did. Princess Portia. That's you, isn't it?"

"Sure, that's me. That's not what I meant, though. It's my marks. They make everyone nervous. I don't want you to feel uncomfortable. Not that you look uncomfortable. I was just checking."

Wow. Babble much?

I decide that now is a great time to look at my sensible shoes and plot my quick escape.

"Portia, look at me."

I slowly lift my gaze. Mystery Man fixes me with a stare that's so intense it could cut diamonds. "Please keep me company."

I've never done drugs, but they might feel something like the rush of happy that those words bring to my soul. "Sure. I can stay."

"Good." His grin returns. My knees go wobbly.

The quiet that follows is somehow comforting. More like a warm blanket than the awkward silence that usually happens when I talk to guys. My gaze lands on his tail. Mom has one like his, as does every decent Arena fighter in Purgatory. "Are you from around here?"

He lets out a low chuckle. "Not in the slightest."

I look at him expectantly.

"You really don't know who I am, do you?" he asks.

My skin turns so red, even my scalp burns with embarrassment. "No. Should I?"

"Come to think of it, no, you shouldn't."

I inspect the man more closely. "Something about you does seem familiar, though." My body feels light as a feather. I'm having a conversation with an actual guy that doesn't involve terror and running away. And hey, I'm even having fun.

Another face pops into my mind. "Do you know my brother, maybe?"

"Everyone knows Maxon." A playful light dances in his eyes. "Guess again."

"Are we making this a game, then?"

"Only if you wish it."

I tap my cheek, pretending to consider this turn of events. "Fine. A guessing game it is."

"Brilliant."

"Let's see. Are you maybe a quasi-demon... But one who's not living in Purgatory?"

He winks. "I'll give you a hint. I'm one of the Furor."

I scrub my hand over my forehead. That makes him a full-blooded dragon shifter. Now, I'm really stumped. I may be part Furor, but I know hardly anything about them. All of a sudden, that seems like a huge miss. "Are you from the Hexenwing tribe of Furor? I know their Level One spells."

The arrowhead end of his tail moves in a 'no' motion. "Wrong color dragon scales."

I snap my fingers, trying to make memories appear. Maxon talked about color schemes for Furor scales. I didn't pay attention. "Don't tell me. Black scales mean you're from the Thornclaw tribe. Or is it Shrillroar?"

Another chuckle. "Neither."

"Okay, I need a hint."

"Why not ask your Mum? Her scales are the same color."

"True." I can't help but laugh. "Wow, I need to take an interest in the after-realms outside of magic."

"Maybe I can help on that score. How about I come round for tea sometime? We can have a chat."

"Tea." My mental gears try to process this. Doesn't happen. He's not scared or running away and now, he's talking about beverages. That doesn't mean what I think it means, does it? "I'm not sure."

"Perhaps you fancy a pint, then?"

"Of ice cream?" Finally, my mental gears start clicking again. "Oh, as in you and me? On a date somewhere?" My eyes almost bug out of my head. "That's not a good idea."

His brows lift ever so slightly, like this conversation is our little secret. "And why's that?"

I know nothing about people in general, let alone men?

"I have a very busy life."

"Doing what?"

"You know. Books. Stuff. Things. It's cooler than it sounds."

Do I seem like a loser or what?

"Quite busy, indeed. Though perhaps you could squeeze in a cuppa." He leans in closer. "In between Stuff and Things."

His attention makes me woozy. The feeling's so

lovely that it takes me a while to process what's happening. I gasp when I realize it. "You're looking at my marks."

"I know. I like them." And the way he says the words, there's no question this time. He means it.

The moment freezes for me. This is a man. A very attractive man. He really likes my marks. I'm not sure whether to cheer or cry. In the end, I shake my head in disbelief. "You like them?"

"Ah, you've no idea how much."

With those words, I go from confusion to all-out panic. This has turned too real, too fast. "I have to go now," I say quickly. "I have, you know, stuff to do." *And I'm terrified out of my skull.*

He nods slowly, and the look in his eyes says 'this isn't over.'

As I rush through Grandpa Xav's office, I hear the Mystery Man call after me. "See you soon, Princess."

Every word sends a happy jolt of anticipation through me.

Oh, I hope so.

Chapter Three

I pace through my penthouse in downtown Purgatory. It's a swanky place with a retro flapper vibe. I've been holed up here for the day or so after my lecture. At least, I think it's been a day. Hard to tell since I've skipped meals, sleep, and personal hygiene. It's all for a good cause, though. I'm about to pinpoint when the Firmament might collapse. Who needs food?

On the tiled floor of my living room, I've drawn a pentagram in yellow chalk and placed enchanted canopic jars inside. I nod once to myself.

Here it comes. I am so nailing the incantation this time.

My mouth starts forming words for the spell, but another kind of magical energy wells up inside me. It's a liquid power that slides along my tongue, contorting it into odd shapes. My words come out strangely.

"Abella sinotro."

Wrong.

"Abella sinatra."

Even more wrong.

"Abella synapse."

What?

I ball my hands into my hair with irritation. That damned force always trips up my tongue. I've only had it checked it out a million times. No one knows what it is, only that it clogs my mouth. *Why can't I chant like a normal witch?*

"I hate you!"

Yes, I'm yelling at an invisible magical force.

Yes, that's kind of crazy.

No, I don't care anymore.

I kick the couch, completely miss the cushioned parts, and end up stubbing my toe, hard. *Okay, that hurt.*

A small bolt of lightning hovers by the archway to the kitchen, grabbing my attention. The brightness is no larger than my palm and whips about like a fish. I smile. My visitor is one of the igni, a tiny supernatural bolt of power that helps move mortal souls to Heaven or Hell. There's only one being in the after-realms who wields these. Most people call her the Great Scala.

I call her Mom.

More igni appear. Soon hundreds swirl in a column. As the tiny bodies float and dive around each other, a wave of sadness binds my heart. Although I should have inherited Mom's power over igni, I didn't.

The column disappears. In its place stands a

woman with wavy auburn hair, bright blue eyes, and a long, black tail. She wears the fitted white robes of the Great Scala.

Mom fixes me with a big smile. "Good morning, baby."

My chest warms with affection. "Morning to you, too."

She scans the floor. "Cool new spell. Will it mess things up if I sit down? I don't want to throw off your mojo."

"It's okay. My mojo needs a breather." I scooch over and Mom slides in beside me. Her spine is ramrod straight as she fixes me with what I call her 'goddess gaze.' This isn't a casual visit. My mother is here for a reason. A tingle of worry crawls up my neck.

"What's up, Mom?"

"I heard about your speech yesterday."

"Oh, that." I slump deeper into the couch. "I didn't see the tabs this morning."

"Some of the photos were pretty good. That kid with the lizard tail was adorable." Mom drums her fingers on the arm of the couch. She didn't come here to talk about the lizard kid.

"But?"

Mom's eyes narrow. "I heard you lost your temper."

I wince with embarrassment. "Yeah, I suppose I did. That Roy guy was so nasty, I couldn't help it. I just got all…" I wave my hands around and try to find the words. Nothing comes to mind.

"Did you get all angry inside?" asks Mom.

"Pretty much."

"Was your blood boiling until you couldn't stand it anymore?" Mom leans forward. "Well?"

Roy's face comes back to me in a flash of memory. My neck tightens into cords of held-in rage. "Sure, I was angry." My voice comes out low and deadly.

"Yes!" Mom's features brighten. "And so you just went with the rage. You told Mister Creeper how you were Marked for the Void, and in that moment, you didn't care about the crowd or the consequences. Am I right?"

I shift uncomfortably in my seat. "Not sure I want to answer that. You know I never lose my temper."

"Just tell me the truth, honey."

"Okay, you're totally right." I picture the reporter's greasy face again and my fists tighten with fury. "I may even have wanted to hurt him a little."

"Oh, baby!" Mom wraps me in a huge embrace. Even her tail gets into the act.

"Wait, what?" I'm so stunned, I don't return the hug.

"I'm so excited for you. Your first uncontrollable rage. I mean, we always knew you were part Furor. Lust and wrath are in your blood. But even as a child, you never got angry about anything. Remember when Maxon's odd friend Uther dropped you on your head by mistake? You didn't even cry, let alone kick him in the kneecaps."

My eyes turn wistful at the memory. Poor Uther. "He was trying some human dance at Maxon's wedding." I raise my hand. "In his defense, I was young and bounced easily."

"See?" Mom points straight at my nose. "That's exactly what I'm talking about. You're always so calm and persistent, no matter what happens." She looks at the floor. "I bet you've been working on this spell for hours."

I glare angrily at the canopic jars, like it's their fault I can't say a basic spell on command. "Try all night long."

"And you never lost patience once, I bet."

"Actually, I did get a little frustrated just now. I even kicked the couch. Stubbed my toe and everything."

"That's great!" Mom claps her hands together at her chin. "We need to encourage this, see where it goes. Boys, maybe?

"How about a change of subject?"

"Fine, I get it." Mom leans forward and sets her elbows on her knees. "Now, what's this spell all about?"

"I'm trying to calculate when the Firmament will collapse."

She lets out a low whistle. "I didn't realize you were still working on that spell. See what I mean? Persistent." She tilts her head. "How will you do that? No magic caster has ever seen the Firmament."

"That's because they all cast the wrong spells."

"Not following, baby."

"It's powerful magic that wants to stay hidden. You'll never get to it through the front door. But the Void attack the Firmament all the time. If I cast a spell to see the Void, then I'll see the Firmament, too. Simple."

"Clever stuff, baby. Can I watch you cast?"

"Sure." Nervous energy twists through my fingers. "I've been trying to get the incantation right for hours. It isn't easy."

"Take your time."

Closing my eyes tight, I focus all my energy on the two words that make up this spell.

"Abelleta sinotree."

My body feels like it could fly away on an internal cloud of joy. At last, I may have pronounced it correctly. I reopen my eyes. A puff of white smoke now covers the floor

It worked.

"Is that what you wanted to happen?" asks Mom.

My chest swells with a sense of pride. "Partly. Give it a second." The air crackles with fresh energy. Another tiny burst of smoke appears as a golden stone materializes on the pentagram. "And that's it."

"What does that rock mean?"

"It's where the Void will strike next." I close my eyes as magical calculations fly through my mind. *41.730538, -93.324695, Colfax, Iowa.* "They're going to hit Earth in about two hours."

Mom stands and brushes off her robes. "In that case, I must return to Antrum. Your father and I can check it out. We'll call it an emergency demon patrol."

I clench my hands into nervous fists. Demon patrol scares me silly. And the thought of meeting the Void? Petrifying. Still, no one else knows how to make the magical calculations. I force the words out of my mouth. "I'll go with you."

Mom's mouth falls open with amazement. "On demon patrol? Really?"

"Yeah, sure. No big deal." *Total lie.* I haven't gone on patrol since I was twelve.

“If you’re sure.”

“Positive.”

Mom beams with joy. “In that case, let’s get suited up.”

Her words bring everything into clearer focus. Demons. Armor. Patrol. And I’ve never killed anything in my life. A ball of fear tightens in my throat. It’s not easy, but somehow, I’m able to speak past it. “Lead the way.”

Chapter Four

My family and I tramp through a rotting cornfield at night. Browned and dried-out stalks tower above us. We look battle ready in our body armor. So far, we've only confronted a few field mice.

I fidget in my leather fighting suit and duster coat. I had to borrow them from my honorary cousin, Hildy. It's not my usual look.

Mom sighs. "I hate to say this, but when do we call 'time of death' on this patrol?"

"Let's give it a few more minutes," says Dad.

Maxon turns into vapor form. "I can float up and take one last look around."

The small hairs on the back of my neck stand on end. "Someone's casting a spell. Let me see if I can figure out what it is." Closing my eyes, I whisper a thrax incantation to detect nearby magic. My lips won't move. The liquid power that ties up my tongue becomes worse than ever.

"What did you find, baby?" asks Mom.

"Nothing yet."

Dad rubs his neck. "I've a meeting of the Earls first thing in the morning." He lets out a disappointed sigh. "I still need to read all the scrolls with their requests."

"One sec," I say. "Let me try another kind of magic." In honor of my Mystery Man, this time I do a Furor detection spell. I nail it after only three tries. A small burst of bright yellow flame erupts between my hands.

"What does that mean?" asks Mom.

"Someone's definitely casting a cloaking spell. They're hiding what's really happening." I stare into the flames, watching Furor dragon runes appear within the fire. Though it's an older dialect, it's one that I know. "They're just North of this spot." I whisper another Furor incantation and the fire disappears.

Dad takes charge. "Maxon, Myla, and I will go in first. Portia, you follow behind. Keep your protection spells handy. I want you to be sure—"

A pack of Void demons burst into view. The monsters are humanoid and huge, with skin that drips black ooze. They've creepy holes for eyes and oversized hands with extra-long claws. Time seems to slow as they rush in.

Void demons. I've finally found them.

My mind short circuits with shock. I'm dimly aware of my family going into battle around me. Maxon conjures small tornadoes to tear the Void into bits. Mom skewers more of the monsters with her tail. Dad ignites his angelfire sword and slices through half a dozen at once.

Usually, demon patrol is frightening. This time, I can't help feeling sad. The Void's cries are pitiful. Desperation lurks in their empty eyes. They seem more desperate than evil.

One hulking creature breaks off from the rest of the pack and heads right for me. Unlike the rest of the Void, this monster radiates menace. Flames blaze in its eyeholes as it closes in.

Hundreds of battle lessons flicker through my brain all at once. I should take a defensive posture. Cast a fireball spell. Throw a nunchuk. Run for my life.

All I can do is stand and stare.

Moonlight glints off the monster's talons as it slams a fist into the side of my head. Hurt explodes inside my skull. I curl onto my knees. The demon wraps its slimy hands around my neck. Pain spikes through my throat.

I brace my muscles, expecting the creature to try snapping my neck. That doesn't happen. Instead, magic wells inside me. It's the same liquid power that usually clogs my tongue. Now, that energy rushes out of me and into the monster. My body freezes with shock. I did not see this coming.

The creature speaks in a rasping gurgle. "I am the Scintillion. You feed me."

Pain burns my throat as more liquid energy rushes into the Scintillion. The monster's gooey limbs solidify. The six-fingered grasp on my throat tightens. I claw desperately at my neck.

Dad's baculum sword appears in my peripheral vision. The flaming blade stabs between the creature's ribs. The Scintillion roars with pain, but doesn't release its grip. The monster's body now looks gooey and slick again.

Dad twists the blade deeper. "Release my daughter."

The monster only tightens his chokehold. My neck feels ready to snap.

"Let go of her," says Mom. She loops her long tail around the monster's throat, yanking it backward with force. The Scintillion lets go of my neck and howls with rage. It glares at me as its body seeps into the ground. Air rushes back into my lungs. I hunch forward, sucking in rough gasps.

Mom kneels beside me, her features tight with concern. "Are you all right, baby?"

"I'll be fine. That monster got away, though."

"We'll get it next time," says Dad. "Now that we know what we're looking for." He sets his hand on my shoulder. "You did well, Portia."

My heart could have wings, I'm so happy. I did well on demon patrol? Who would have thunk it? "Thanks, Dad."

Maxon motions to us. "You've got to see this." We follow his lead to a clearing. My mouth falls open in shock.

The Void have carved a huge crater into the middle of the cornfield. Massive tree roots sit inside, their surfaces shining with golden light. My heartbeat skyrockets. After all these years, I'm seeing it at last.

The Firmament.

Maxon points to the opposite side of the crater. "Check it out. That's where the Void were chowing down."

Black bite-marks cover the gleaming root. I'd hoped the Void only made a small wound in the flesh of the tree, but that's not the case. Their bites are poisonous. With each passing second, more of the tree's life-glow sickens and fades. I carefully scan the light levels and run some fast calculations. I'd never imagined the Firmament being so dark. My heart jumps into my throat. At this rate of decay, the Firmament won't last long.

This is bad. Very bad.

"The Firmament's in worse shape than I thought." I turn to Maxon. "You have to get us out of here. Now."

"You got it, sis." With a wave of his arm, Maxon creates a cloud of smoke. The haze slowly lifts us above the ground. Ear-splitting cracks echo out from the crater. Boulders break loose from the walls and smash onto the gleaming roots.

The crater collapses into the earth, leaving behind an even larger sinkhole. The dark hole is like a black eye on the landscape. All I can do is stare in shock. The world takes on a dreamlike gleam.

"It's happening," I whisper.

The after-realms are falling apart.

The billions of humans on the Earth are a drop in the bucket compared to the souls in Heaven, the ghouls in the Dark Lands, and even the demons in Hell. All of them will be destroyed without the Firmament.

I sway from foot to foot, my head swimming with the realization. It's one thing to suspect a big kaboom will take down your world. It's quite another to see it happen before your eyes. A chilly cloak of shock presses in around me. This can't be real.

Maxon sets us all down a few yards from the sinkhole's edge. "The humans will lose it when they see this," he says. "They won't be able to explain it away with their science."

"We'll figure out some way to hide it," says Dad. "We always do."

Mom turns to me. "I'm more concerned about what this means for the after-realms. How much trouble are we in, Portia?"

There's no sugar coating this. "Serious trouble. The after-realms could fall apart." A chill of fear rolls up my body.

"How soon?" asks Dad.

"Weeks. Maybe days."

My father's features harden. "We need to gather everyone together and come up with a plan."

I raise my hand halfway. "I really think we should—"

"One minute, Portia." Dad's words are dismissive. It's the way he'd talk to a guard or an earl, or anyone who's not critical to the problem at hand. My family is in crisis mode, and I've never had a serious part to play in that. Bands of frustration tighten my chest. I need to have a voice here, for all our sakes.

Dad punches some keys on the handheld strapped to his wrist. "I'm not getting any read from Antrum."

"Do you think the sinkhole affected the thrax?" asks Mom.

"Yeah," says Maxon. "Could've gotten all the after-realms."

"It *did* impact all the after-realms," I say.

No one responds to me. Dad keeps punching into

his handheld while Mom and Maxon debate what to do next. This is my area of expertise and it's like I'm invisible. My hands clench into fists. I can't let this happen.

Firming up my spine, I speak in a louder voice. "Look, guys—"

"Damn," says Maxon. "I forgot about the elementals. I need to check on them."

"Go," says Dad. "We'll regroup at the Hearth." The Hearth is our family home in Purgatory. It's where we always meet when trouble goes down. "We need status reports on the after-realms. Come find us when you're ready."

Maxon nods and disappears. The moment he's gone, the electronic wail of sirens slices the night air.

"We've got to get moving," says Dad. He takes off into the night and we follow. My body is on autopilot. The whole scene is surreal.

"Sorry, baby," Mom looks back over her shoulder at me as we run along. "You were trying to say something before? Your father and I hit a groove when there's an emergency. We didn't mean to cut you off."

Anger flares inside me. It burns out my dazed mood and puts everything in focus. Suddenly, I don't care how things were done before. They need to take me seriously now.

I pick up speed until we're running side by side. "I've studied the Void for years. I know you all get in your crisis-groove, but I think you need to really listen to what I have to tell you."

"Sure, baby," she says quickly. "Of course. We'll talk about it at the Hearth."

I frown. That's not the heartfelt acknowledgment of teamwork that I was hoping for. Saving the after-realms will be hard enough without having to fight to get every insight across to my family.

The weight of every life in the after-realms presses around me until it's hard to breathe. I know how my family works: fight first and ask questions later. But fighting the Void won't be enough. We have to focus on rebuilding the Firmament. I only hope I can get them to listen before it's too late.

Chapter Five

Mom, Dad, Walker, and I all wait in the main room of the Hearth. Computer equipment is stacked on our massive credenza. Mom fiddles with monitors. Dad types into a keyboard. Walker crawls around under the table, connecting up a nest of wires. He's a ghoul, family friend, and all-around genius when it comes to anything engineering-related. Right now, he's getting us tapped into information feeds from across the after-realms.

"Anything new from Antrum?" I ask. No one says anything. This is the third time that's happened. I realize they're worried and in crisis mode, but it's getting on my nerves.

Mom steps to Dad's side. "Is Antrum coming online?"

I huff out a shocked breath. *Was I dreaming when I asked that question just now?*

One of Dad's monitors flickers to life, casting odd

shadows onto his face. “Information’s feeding in now. Minor quakes shook up two of the outlying houses. We’re sending in casters from Striga to fix things.”

Walker reconnects more wires. “Does that do it, Linc?”

My father stares at a dark monitor. “Nope.”

Walker sighs and pinches the bridge of his nose. “Purgatory information feed… Purgatory information feed… Where else can I tap in?” Like all ghouls, Walker is crazy-tall with colorless skin and a pronounced bone structure. He’s also part angel and a total sweetie.

I jam my hands in my pockets and pace the room. So far, Earth, Antrum, Heaven, and Hell have all checked in. Every realm has reported damage. Nothing too terrible, though. We’re still waiting on news from the outlying sectors of Purgatory and the Elementals. Normally, Purgatory would be first to give us an update. We saw some emergency vehicles on our way over, but nothing serious. And the com grid is down, so there’s no knowing what’s really happening. A sinking feeling seeps into my bones. All the magic of the Firmament connects into Purgatory. By my calculations, it could get hit the worst.

Footsteps thump along the roof. There’s only one person who does that. Pops just landed, which means there was at least some damage in Purgatory. Pops doesn’t fly around angel-style if he can avoid it. The public goes nuts, not to mention the paparazzi.

I stare at the winding corkscrew-style steps that lead from the roof to the first floor, anxious to see Pops. He’s been around since the dawn of time. Nothing rattles him, and I need that strength right now. However, the first person to appear on the staircase isn't Pops. It's Gram in her classic purple suit. They must have flown over together. She scans the room carefully.

"Everyone all right?" asks Gram. "We heard the reports of an earthquake on demon patrol."

"Oh, we're fine," says Mom. "Portia stood her ground against a Class A demon." Mom shoots me a thumbs-up, and I fairly burst with pride. "What's happening in the rest of Purgatory? Why can't we get any read out?"

"I'd call it an earthquake," says Gram. "But it wasn't. Six blocks simply collapsed into the ground. Worst sinkhole we've ever seen."

A weight of worry slips off my shoulders. Losing six blocks is tough. Not as bad as it could have been, though.

Pops steps down the stairs, catches my eye, and winks. "How's my angel girl?"

"I'm fine, Pops." Relief trickles through me. It's good to see Pops looking so calm in his gray suit. Like always, he has cocoa skin, black hair and a white-toothed smile. He saves his wings for special occasions. Even so, there's no questioning the aura of angelic power that follows him wherever he goes.

Dad nods toward Pops. "You don't seem worried."

"Let's see," says Pops. "The quasi population will be without television for a few hours while we reroute the power grid. No one got seriously hurt. All in all, I've seen much worse."

Confidence warms my heart. Pops is unflappable.

Walker fiddles with some more wires from his

spot under the credenza. "Are we getting anything now?" he asks.

Dad claps his hands. "That's it. Purgatory info feed is up and running."

"Didn't even take us a few hours," says Pops.

While everyone huddles around the newly live monitor, I watch their activity from across the room. It's official. I've returned to my usual role in a crisis. Watch from afar. Make sure Mom eats something. Grab some extra research if there's magic involved. This is wrong. I've spent too long studying the Void to stand aside now. But I'm not leadership material, am I?

A puff of smoke pours out of the fireplace and takes the shape of Maxon. Like the rest of us, he's in his demon-fighting outfit. The group that's huddled around the computers stops talking.

"How's everything with the Elementals?" asks Dad.

"Fine," says Maxon. "They don't experience the after-realms like mortals do. They hardly noticed a thing." He shrugs. "I'm still trying to wrap my brain around how to rule them. Humans dump trash in a lake and they want me to kill every last mortal. The after-realms go unstable and they could care less."

Mom's features brighten. "How's Lianna?"

"Getting the earth elementals under control. My girl's a badass." He gestures around the room. "You all fine here?"

"Everything's under control," says Dad. "You can take off."

"In that case, I'll..." Maxon pauses, listening. A light scraping sound echoes from the roof.

Maxon frowns. "No way."

"Is someone else landing?" I ask.

"Oh, yeah," says Maxon.

"Who is it?" asks Mom.

My brother beams with joy. "My buddy T is here."

At this point, my Mom does something I've never seen her do before. Primp. She turns toward the wall mirror, fluffs out her hair, and pinches her cheeks. Even Grandma Cam makes sure her suit is smooth and all the buttons are done up. She's definitely in Presidential mode now. A sneaking suspicion crawls up my spine.

Someone's landed on the roof. It can't be the Mystery Man, can it?

I dismiss the idea out of hand. I've been obsessing about this guy on and off for the last two days. Plenty of people fly around and land on rooftops. Just because someone's here doesn't make it the Mystery Man.

Only I sure hope it's him.

My body freezes with anticipation as heavy footfalls sound from the upper stairs. Bit by bit, our new visitor steps down the spiral stairs. At first, I see his biker boots and worn jeans. After that, I can make out a solid chest, black Henley, and crazy-wide shoulders. Finally, there's his angular bone structure, five o'clock shadow, and tousled black hair.

Every nerve cell in my body goes on alert. It's him. My guy. Not sure when I decided ownership, but there it is. Mine.

Maxon wraps my guy in a big hug. "T? What're you doing here? I haven't seen you since…"

My guy's mouth quirks with a grin. "Since your

wedding."

Maxon rubs his neck and winces. "Yeah, well. Lianna and me have been real busy running the Elementals."

"I understand," my guy says. "I can visit you too, you know."

Maxon lets out one of his rumbling chuckles. "Yeah, what's up with that?"

"I've had things on my mind." My guy's gaze locks on me from across the room. A hot blush crawls up my neck.

For a few seconds, Maxon only looks between his friend and me. At length, my brother's eyes narrow with suspicion. I wince. Are my feelings for the Mystery Man that obvious?

"What brings you here, T?" Maxon's voice drops an octave. "Or should I say, who?"

My blush deepens. I guess my feelings are pretty obvious, after all.

The Mystery Man waves his hand. He's the picture of smooth, and I can't help liking him for that. Correction, like him *more* for that.

"There are sinkholes popping up all over Furonium," says my guy. "Does your family have any news to share, by chance?"

Of course, he came here. If there's a major crisis in the after-realms, my family is involved. I don't know how it happens, only that it does. Always.

Maxon chuckles. "Now, what makes you think that *we're* in the know?"

"Because you always are." The guy turns to Walker, my parents, and grandparents. "But your knickers aren't in a twist, so I can only guess that whatever it is, it isn't too terrible."

"It's not bad at all," says Grandma Cam with a giggle.

Giggle? I do a double take. Yes, my grandmother actually giggled while in Presidential mode. Unbelievable.

My guy steps up to Gram. "Madame President, great to see you."

"And to see you, too," says Gram. She giggles even more loudly this time.

It takes everything I have not to push my own grandmother on her ass and tell her to back off. I pinch the bridge of my nose, not believing the feelings that are coursing though me. What humiliating compulsion is next? Challenging Gram to a duel?

Next, my guy turns to my parents. "Your Highnesses."

"Always a pleasure," says Mom.

Fresh jealousy courses through me. *Unbelievable.*

With each person that my guy addresses, he gets closer to talking to me. I nervously shift my weight from foot to foot. Nothing he says clues me in to his real identity, although I suspect that my brain isn't functioning too well right now. In fact, the logical side of my head is pounding on the back of my skull about something. I have a feeling that this man's identity should be obvious, if I could only focus again. But that's not happening.

The guy turns to Pops. "General, we keep missing each other."

Pops' eyes narrow just like Maxon's did a minute ago. "You don't say."

Now, I know that look on Pops. He's totally been

avoiding my guy. That makes me irrationally angry. My hands clench into the leather of my duster. One nail pops through the super-charged and supposedly unbreakable fabric. I don't care.

"Nothing to worry about," replies my guy smoothly. "I've become an expert at waiting on your balcony."

"So I've heard." My grandfather inspects me carefully, and I feel like he can see straight through me, unpeeling every secret I've ever had. This is about more than Pops not liking my guy. No, my grandfather's figured out my obsession with the Mystery Man. Now that he knows the truth, what will happen? Knowing my family, it will be extremely embarrassing. A dozen thoughts fly through my brain at once.

Run for your life.

Stand perfectly still.

Say something flirty.

Pretend you have a migraine.

Pressing my lips together, I pick at the buttons on my duster. It's not my best plan, but it's a plan.

My guy steps up to Walker. "We haven't met."

Walker offers his hand. "I'm Walker, majordomo to the ghouls who rule the Dark Lands."

"The way I hear it, you effectively rule the Dark Lands solo." My guy laughs, and it's a lovely, rolling sound. "Am I right?"

Walker chuckles. "Shh. Don't tell. The Oligarchy are easier to manage when they think they're in charge."

My guy starts up again. "And I'm…"

For a blissful moment, I think I may discover his

identity, but Walker breaks up the conversation.

"I know who you are," says Walker.

And the blissful moment is over.

My guy then strides across the room, his gaze locked with mine. My pulse races with excitement. He pauses before me. A chill runs across my skin as I become overly aware of my form-fitting and very leather fighting outfit. I should feel exposed. Somehow, I don't. My guy scans me from head to toe. Twice. The attention feels glorious.

A little bubble forms around me and my Mystery Man. It's like there's no one else in the room. My brain buzzes with happiness. It's all I can do to get out one word. "Hi."

"Hullo, luv."

"I don't usually dress this way. In case you're wondering."

Shut up, Portia.

A small smile rounds his full mouth. "You're a beauty in anything."

"Thanks." I twist my fingers together nervously. "I've never been called a beauty before."

"Glad I could change that."

"Hey there," says Maxon. With a puff of smoke, he dematerializes from his spot by the fireplace, only to re-poof himself right between me and Mister Mystery. Suddenly, I feel hyper-aware of all the eyes staring at me. Awkwardness presses all around my body, like physical weights against my skin.

While Maxon blocks me from my guy, the rest of my family glares at Mister Mystery like he just mauled me on the carpet.

"T, this is my *sister* Portia." Maxon shoots me a

meaningful look. "You know him?"

It's hard to speak when you're suddenly too amped up to breathe. "Kind of."

"We've never been formally introduced," says my guy.

"Oh." Maxon exhales with relief. "That explains a lot."

Here it comes.

"You don't know who he is, Portia?" asks Gram from across the room.

"It's me, guys," I say, and my voice is a little short. "Being Marked for the Void takes up a lot of my time."

Yow. Did that come out of my mouth? Why yes, yes it did. I scan the room. Everyone stares at me like I just sprouted an extra head. It's not a bad kind of feeling, actually.

"Oh," says Grandma Cam. She presses her lips together firmly. I'm about to give myself some mental high fives for having shut up anyone in my family ever when Maxon gently touches my shoulder.

"Portia," he says. "This is Emperor Tempest."

My mouth falls open. Again. I say nothing. Again.

The words echo through my mind in odd ways. *Emperor Tempest? As in, the ruler of all Furor?* This guy is *the* greater demon of lust and wrath. No one beats him in battle, and he's notorious for taking new lovers like clockwork. No wonder I felt such an overwhelming attraction to him after only one glance. Causing obsessive behavior is his job.

Wow, I'm totally out of my league here.

Maxon fairly drags Tempest back to the rest of my family. "You came here to talk about the sinkholes, yeah?"

Anger heats my blood. I don't need Maxon protecting me like some child. My family either, for that matter. When I speak, my voice has a sharp edge to it. "Maxon, I thought you had to go home to Lianna."

"Nah, I'm good." Maxon doesn't look at me when he replies. That only happens when he's really irritated about something. My jaw clenches with frustration.

"It's like this," says Maxon to Tempest. "The Firmament is in bad shape. The first thing we have to do is stop the Void."

"Not the first thing," I say. No one looks at me.

Except Tempest.

"You're our foremost expert on the Void," says Tempest. "Why don't you come closer? Maybe everyone will hear you better if you stand by the table."

"She's fine where she is," says Maxon quickly.

I grit my teeth so hard, I'm surprised I don't chip a molar. Did I just get dismissed again?

"What's important is this," says Maxon. "We know how to find the Void now. We can take them down."

"Let me guess," says Tempest. "You want to raise an army."

I roll my eyes. Here it comes. My family is very pro-military. They've all spent years raising warriors for battle. Too bad that tactic won't work here. "Guys, you have to listen."

Maxon looks between Tempest and me. "Portia, I get that you want attention now."

I inhale a shocked breath. *Did my brother really say that to me?* "No, Maxon. This isn't about me. It's about the information you need to make a good decision. Destroying the Void will work over the long haul, but we don't have time to focus on that now." I'd say that it feels wrong to kill them, but I know that'd go over like a lead balloon. "First things first. We must rejuvenate the Firmament. Get more power in there."

"And how do we do that?" asks Tempest.

It takes me a few seconds to process that I actually got a follow-up question.

How do we do that?

A pleasant shiver runs down my spine. This guy is the Emperor of the Furor and he's looking at me like my opinion counts. No, more than counts. It's like I'm the most important person in the room. My chest warms with pride.

Maxon's mouth tightens into a protective line. "Why are you asking her?"

I shoot Maxon a hurt look. Tempest was treating me like an equal, not a piece of the furniture. I don't need to be protected from that. If anything, I need more of it in my life.

"As I said, Portia's the expert on the Void." Tempest's gaze meets mine again. "You were saying?"

For some reason, it's easy to speak my mind while Tempest has me locked in his encouraging gaze. "We need to go to the Grove. That's where the Sacred Trees are, the ones whose roots and branches make up the Firmament. If there's any way to save the after-realms, that's where it'll happen. Rejuvenate those trees and that buys us time to kill the Void."

"Okay," says Mom. "Let's say that's the plan." She gestures to me. "Do you know where to find the Grove?"

"No," I say quietly. "It took me years to find a spell to track the Void. We don't have that kind of time left now."

Dad hops to his feet. "Which is why we need to raise an army right away. If we use maximum force, we can destroy at least some of the Void. If nothing else, it'll slow the damage to the Firmament."

Tempest rakes his hand through his shaggy, black hair. "I know how to find the Grove."

My mouth falls open with shock. I can count on one finger the people who are actively researching the Grove right now. That would be me. And here, Tempest knows where it is? Who is this guy?

"You can get to the Grove?" asks Pops. "People have been trying since the beginning of time. I've been told that it's impossible."

"And I've been told that the Grove doesn't exist," adds Gram.

"Oh, it exists all right," says Tempest. "It's hidden under Purgatory's Gray Sea. I've never been inside, although I know how to get there."

Everyone starts talking at the same time.

"What?"

"How?"

"Who told you?"

I take another step away from the commotion. All of a sudden, I'm not so sure I want to know the answers to these questions. Tempest just made me feel like my opinion mattered. It's stupid, but that meant something to me. But if he knew about the

Grove and never told anyone? That's a big miss in my opinion. Something doesn't add up.

Maxon's voice rises over the din. "Come on, T. You sure it wasn't a long night and too much angelflower wine?"

"Positive," says Tempest. "And I can find it again." His gaze darkens. "But I must bring Portia with me. Alone."

At this point, two sides of me break into all-out war. First, there's logical me. That tells me to run from Tempest and fast. All this weird stuff about the Grove and now he wants me alone? Agreeing to that is dumb with a capital D.

But then, there's my heart. It's thumping up a storm at the thought of being alone with Tempest. Suppose the way he's acting is real? Maybe he does think my opinion matters. He might even be the kind of guy who can see beyond my marks.

At last, my logical side kicks in with a vengeance. Tempest can get me in to the Grove. The after-realms are falling apart. So what if Tempest is a little shady? I have billions of lives on the line here.

If there's any hope that I can get answers and fix the Firmament, then I'm in.

When I speak, my voice comes out loud and steady. "I'm going with Tempest."

"No, we're all going," says Dad, and the stern look on his face says that's not up for discussion.

Tempest nods. "Tomorrow at dusk, then. We'll meet at Pyramid Rock in the Gray Sea." He stomps up the spiral staircase and leaves without waiting for a reply.

I watch him go and somehow, I'm certain of one

thing. Even if we do find a way to save the after-realms, my life will never be the same again.

# # #

My family has been having the time of their lives, running battle plans for over an hour now. I've decided to raid the freezer. I'm about to grab a pint of rocky road when Maxon materializes beside me.

"Glad I caught you alone. We need to talk about T."

My mouth thins to an angry line. "That's none of your business."

"Hey, I'm just trying to do the right thing here. You do realize that T's a greater demon, yeah?"

I keep staring at the contents of the freezer like the meaning of life is hidden in there. Much as I hate Maxon's barging in, I can't help being curious about what he has to say. I can't shake that odd feeling that Tempest is hiding something. "I'm aware of what Tempest is."

"Then, there you have it. Stay away from him." Maxon scans the walls, the floor, and the countertop… Anything but me. I know my brother enough to realize that there's something he isn't telling me here. That's his guilty look.

"That's it?" I ask.

"Yeah."

"That's not very convincing. There's a lot of gray area when it comes to demons. Look at the Queen of Hell. Nefer is a good ruler."

Maxon sighs. "Fine. I know the guy. The real Tempest. He is what his father made him, and that

Furor was a freak named Chimera. You heard of him?"

"A little. Chimera didn't rule for long and had a thing about cleansing the Furor so there are only pureblood dragons left. He killed a lot of Furorling." A chill creeps over my skin. What must it have been like for Tempest to be raised by a guy like that?

"Well, Chimera was best buds with Armageddon, the old King of Hell. They even shared torture techniques."

"Oh." My heart sinks to my toes. A torture expert and he was Tempest's father.

"It's like this. When Armageddon abducted me, it fucked me up for decades, and the freak only had me less than seven days. Chimera tortured Tempest for years on end. T is a whole new level of screwed up. There's only so far away from that he can go, you know what I mean?"

"All too well. I know what it's like to have people judge you because of how you look or what they've heard about you." *I need to make my own decisions about Tempest.*

"Don't get me wrong. T is charming, but the guy practically invented 'hit it and quit it.' He goes for women who know the score and want the best night of their lives. But that's not you. You're going to get attached to him and when he moves on, it'll break your heart. I won't see that happen to you."

It was just a few days ago I curled up in a ball on the couch because the dry cleaner guy was scared of me. Imagine if I spent time with Tempest... Or we kissed. I'd be a basket case. I inhale a shaky breath. "I don't want to see that, either."

"You watch yourself, yeah?"

"Yeah."

"Good call." Maxon brushes a kiss against my cheek and then mists away.

Once he's gone, I decide to eat my weight in ice cream. Or at least as much as I can shovel in before the world falls apart.

Chapter Six

I'm halfway into my first pint when the floor of the Hearth starts shaking. Small figurines crash onto the floor. Bits of plaster cascade from the ceiling like snowflakes.

Walker hops to his feet. "It's another sinkhole!"

"Get the equipment," says Mom.

Walker closes his eyes and a black, door-sized hole opens up to his right. A ghoul portal. This is how ghouls transport themselves from one side of the after-realms to the other.

Walker steps into the portal, disappears, and returns just as quickly. "I found us a stable spot. We've got to get the gear out."

"Good." Dad starts unplugging equipment left and right. "Walker and I will link up. Portia, you hand the equipment through the portal. Myla, you grab it on the other side."

Adrenaline pumps through my body at double

speed. We can't lose our connection to the after-realms. I also don't want the Hearth to fall down a sinkhole, but we have bigger things to worry about right now.

We quickly create a daisy chain. Dad and Walker link elbows. Mom waits on the opposite side to act as catcher. I'm the pitcher in this scenario, so it's my job to pass stuff to Mom through the portal.

I quickly unplug all the equipment and hoist the first box of tech. "Ready?" I ask.

"Pass it through," says Dad.

I press the large box into the darkness. I feel the tug on the other side as Mom picks up the equipment. I let go and the box disappears.

"Did it work?" I ask.

"Yup," says Dad. "Keep going." His features strain with effort. Even with Walker's help, keeping a ghoul portal open this long is a huge physical drain.

I glance at the dozen monitors, routers, servers, and boxes of wires that now lay on the floor. Another tremor convulses the room. I grab the next item in line—a monitor—and pass it through to Mom. A few data servers follow.

Nine more to go.

The Hearth lurches around us again. Beads of sweat drip down my father's cheek. Hairline fractures appear in the wall. Panic charges me with energy. I focus on passing the routers and servers next; anything that transmits data. Mom grabs them from me in quick succession.

Only three boxes remain.

Another heave strikes the building. The floorboards snap beneath our feet. Dad loses his footing and grabs the edge of the ghoul portal. "Portia! Reach through. Grab your mother's hand."

Leaning forward, I grasp into the darkness. There's no familiar tug on the other side. "I don't feel Mom anymore. Are you still in contact with Walker?"

"He's got my right hand." Dad fixes me with a serious look. "I need you to listen to me carefully. Grab my wrist and hold on tight. I'll pull us both through."

An ear-splitting rumble sounds as the floor heaves once again. Chunks of ceiling plaster tumble in. A figure swoops in through the opened ceiling hole, its identity masked by dust and debris. My pulse skyrockets.

"I can't reach Mom," I say. "Let go, Dad. I'll find another way out."

Dad's face strains red with effort. His fingertips turn white with the pressure of holding onto the edge of the ghoul portal. "Not good enough. Grab my wrist."

The figure steps out of the debris. It's Tempest. He's in his human form, dressed in black. White light shimmers across his shoulders as his dragon wings appear behind his shoulders. They're long, black, and reach almost to the ground. Tempest steps to my side.

"I've got her, Your Highness."

Dad's gaze locks with mine, his features wild with worry. "I want you with your family. Take my—" But Dad finally loses his grip on the portal. He disappears into the darkness. I gasp with shock. On reflex, I reach toward him. Tempest grabs my hands, pulling me backward.

"We're getting you out of here." He says. "Now."

In one smooth motion, Tempest hoists me into his arms. His dragon wings rustle down his back before spreading wide, ready for flight. I ball my hand into his shirt and hold on tight.

The walls crumble. Huge chunks of plaster fall to the floor. Ceiling beams break free, tearing down a knot of wires. Sparks fly. The curtains burst into flame. I wince as a volley of hot sparks flies at my face.

Tempest's wings beat in a speedy rhythm as we lift from the floor. We quickly rise through the new hole in the ceiling. Below me, the Hearth collapses in on itself. My limbs numb with shock. Every last bit of my childhood home—the floorboards and walls, the picture frames and teaspoons—tumbles into the ground. Glass crashes. Metal snaps. Furniture gets pulverized. Panic spikes through my nervous system. Suddenly, I can't pull enough air into my lungs.

Tempest curls me more tightly against his chest. His firm arms encircle me, cocooning me in safety. His heartbeat keeps a steady rhythm against my cheek. My breathing slows. I even loosen my death grip on his shirt. Tempest's voice sounds deep and gentle in my ear. "Are you all right, Portia?"

"I'm fine." And strangely enough, that's the truth. Something about Tempest feels as solid and familiar as my books.

We rise higher in the air. The cookie cutter suburban landscape stretches out in every direction. The knot of worry in my chest loosens. There are no more sinkholes other than my parent's place.

"What do you want to do?" asks Tempest.

"Go to the Grove. Save the after-realms." I add one last word, my voice tight with urgency. "Now."

Chapter Seven

Tempest scoops me in his arms and we take off in a new direction. I don't need to ask where we're headed. The Gray Sea isn't far from here, and that's where Tempest said we'd find the entrance to the Grove.

I rest my head against his chest and catch my breath. "Thank you."

"For what, luv?"

"Coming back for me."

"Of course. Dragons have highly developed senses of smell and hearing. I hadn't gotten far when I heard another sinkhole coming. I turned around the moment I knew. I'm only surprised…" He shakes his head.

"Only surprised about what?"

"I thought you'd want me to take you to your family. They have very strong ideas about how to solve things, and I know you're all very close."

"We are, but not when it comes to this. If we met up with them, I'd spend more time convincing them to listen to me than actually saving the after-realms."

I hadn't noticed that we'd crossed from the residential area to the Gray Sea. Now that Tempest's started to descend, I can't miss the huge swath of charcoal-colored sand beneath us. Tempest arches his wings and we spiral down onto the warm desert.

"We're here," says Tempest. He sets me on my feet and I immediately miss his touch. With another flash of light, the wings vanish from Tempest's shoulders. I look away when he catches me staring.

"Thanks again," I say quickly. "Now, if you'll show me the door to the Grove, you can be on your way."

Tempest's features turn unreadable. "What?"

Every cell in my body wants me to beg him to help. I can't ask that of the Emperor of the Furor, though. He has responsibilities other than my schemes to salvage the Firmament.

I grip my hands together anxiously at my waist. "You have your own realm to worry about, Tempest. Someone marked up my face. This must sound crazy, but I think I'm supposed to fix the Firmament."

Tempest's gaze softens. "That's not crazy."

I puff out a relieved breath. "Whatever it is, it's my problem, not yours." I take a pointed step away from him. "Take care of your people, Tempest. Open the door to the Grove and go. You've done enough."

Tempest steps closer until our bodies are only inches apart. "First of all, I wouldn't be much of a ruler if I didn't have smart leaders on my team. And second, I am not leaving you, Portia."

My mind blanks. This news is a shock to my system. "You're not?"

Tempest cups my chin in his hand. "Never." He runs his thumb over my bottom lip. I shiver. "Do we understand each other?"

I stare at him, at a total loss for words. He can't mean never as in never, ever. This is just until the quest is over, right? And hey, we might not even live that long. Still, whatever he's promising, I'll take it. I need all the help I can get. Relief winds around me, secure as a blanket. "I understand, Tempest."

"Good." He looks into my eyes again, and that intense stare returns. "Ready to open the door to the Grove?"

"I'm ready."

Tempest begins a low chant in dragon tongue, the sounds snarling and deep. One word repeats over and over with a gentle lilt. *Rhana*. His incantation rings through the air in odd ways. I don't know all of what he says. I can translate enough to know that he's getting ready to open a door of some kind. The atmosphere crackles with magic.

I tilt my head, surprised. I'd expected a lot of things on this crazy quest. Somehow the fact that Tempest would be a wizard was not one of them. At all. He finishes and bows his head.

"You know magic," I say breathlessly.

Tempest shrugs. "When you become a greater demon, you gain all sorts of interesting skills. For me, magic was one such surprise." He inhales deeply. "Your Furor blood responds to it, you know."

"What do you mean?" My eyes grow big with surprise. "I smell?"

Tempest offers me his crooked smile, the one that warms me to my toes. "Nothing unpleasant, luv. Your magic reaches out to mine."

I shake my head. "Your dragon feelers are off on that one. When I cast, I use words. There is some kind of magic in me, but it doesn't reach out to anyone. It just locks up my words." I wince. "I realize that may sound crazy."

"No, not at all." He looks at me like I just solved the secrets of the universe. "Quite insightful, I'd say."

His words warm my soul. Here I am, a woman starved for attention and he's handing me a five-course meal of praise. This can't be real. I gesture awkwardly at the desert, anxious to change the subject. "We should get to the Grove."

"As you command." When he speaks again, Tempest's voice booms across the empty desert. "I stand here today, the dragon Tau Epsilon Omicron Theta, Supreme Chieftain of the Firelord tribe, Emperor of the Furor, and Gatherer of the Marked. I demand the Grove open for me."

A small pit appears in the desert floor. A flight of steps leads down into the darkness.

"Safer if we walk side by side," says Tempest. "That okay, luv?"

"That's fine."

Together, we head down into the mysterious Grove. With every step, I feel the weight of the after-realms fall more squarely on my shoulders. So many people are counting on me now. *Please, let me have the strength to help them.*

Chapter Eight

Tempest and I follow a winding passageway that's made from rough-hewn earth. Bits of root and rock jut out from the walls. The scent of fresh soil hangs in the air.

After a few turns, the tunnel opens onto a large underground chamber. The place looks totally deserted. More fresh earth lines the floor and ceiling. A forest of dead trees stretches off into the shadows.

I wince. The smell of decay lingers here. A shiver of unease runs down my spine. That stench is a sure sign of the Void. Could the Scintillion be here, too? I rub my neck, remembering the monster's chokehold. "Do you think the Void are waiting for us?"

"It's likely. Stay close."

Beneath our feet, the root ends slither around like snakes. Within seconds, they realign into a glowing pathway. I inhale a shocked breath. Talk about rolling out the red carpet. "Guess someone knows we're here."

"Rather dodgy." Tempest scans the shadows, his full mouth tightening into a frown. "I don't like it. Stay close, luv."

Tempest and I follow the bright trail through the dead forest. It ends in a round clearing that holds four massive trees. A golden glow dances in their bark. Huge roots bore into the soil; hefty branches poke into the earthen ceiling.

Magic pools around and inside everything. The force is liquid, powerful, and turns my skin into gooseflesh. Tempest and I step closer to the four great trees. Each one is as wide around as I am tall.

"The Sacred Trees," I whisper.

"Yes," says Tempest, his voice tight.

"What's wrong?"

"My dragon is on edge. We aren't alone."

A man steps out from behind one of the massive trees. "Hey, there."

I take one look at this guy and then blink hard. No way can this be real.

The stranger is tall and fit with a picture-perfect tan. He's totally my type, what with his short blond hair, bright blue eyes, and thousand-watt smile. He even has khaki pants with pleats. The sleeves of his white button down are rolled up to his elbows.

"I'm Alden. Pleasure to meet you." The guy steps closer and what I see makes me gasp. He has tribal marks around his right eye. They're just like mine, only his are white.

I stare at him, open mouthed. "What? How?"

"I know, I know," he says with a laugh. "Pretty crazy, right? I'm one of the Marked, too." Alden turns to Tempest. "And you must be her Gatherer."

Tempest nods. Alden offers me his hand. "Pleased to meet you, too, uh…"

"Portia." I shake Alden's hand. The touch sends a rush through me. Or more accurately, out of me. Liquid energy flows from my body into his. I pull back my hand like it's on fire. "What was that?"

Alden shoots me a puzzled look. "Don't you know? I'm the last Marked. I've done what I can for the Firmament. Now my magic's tapped out. You're here to replace me."

My skin still tingles in strange ways. "That doesn't explain what just happened."

"I used to carry Firmament energy inside me, just like you do now. But I finished my quest and sent all my power into the Sacred Trees. I'm running on empty these days. Guess I took a little charge off you by mistake." His blue eyes narrow with suspicion. "How come you don't know any of this stuff?"

"I study the Firmament," I say slowly. "I've never found any information about the rules of being Marked."

"Of course not. We're a super-secret society," says Alden. "But your Gatherer was supposed to prep you on everything."

I stare at Tempest. My mouth hangs open with surprise. He called himself my Gatherer when he opened the door. "You knew about all this?"

"I'm your Gatherer. It's my job to know."

His answer stings. "Why didn't you tell me?"

"I shared everything I could, Portia. My instructions were followed to the letter." Tempest's eyes glisten with intensity. "You have to believe me."

I shiver under the strength of his stare. Only a few

minutes ago, I was cradled in Tempest's arms, feeling cozy and safe. *Was that my lonely mind creating someone who wasn't really there?* A sad weight settles into my stomach. "It's hard to know what to believe."

Alden steps between us. "Look, we don't have much time." He turns his thousand-watt smile on Tempest. "Thanks for gathering her here, man. Great work. You can show yourself out whenever you're ready."

My breath catches. "Show himself out?"

Alden shrugs. "Yeah, the Gatherer never goes on the quest."

My revolving opinions on Tempest take another turn. Whatever he did or didn't say, I feel better with Tempest along. "Not this time. He goes with us."

"That's not how we do things," says Alden. He tilts his head, considering. "But sure, if it makes you feel better, he can come along for a while. Help us get started."

Tempest folds his arms over his chest. The sleeves of his leather jacket creak ominously with the motion. "What things are we starting?"

"The quest," says Alden.

"Any more specifics?"

Alden's tan complexion loses some color. "We've got to rush. Let's talk about it on the way."

I frown. "I'm with Tempest on this. I'd like to know what we're supposed to do."

"Sure, fine." Alden laughs again. This time, it comes out a little too loud and forced. "Portia is Marked, just like me. We were chosen by the Firmament to carry its power. Our job is to open four seedpods, one for each of the Sacred Trees." He counts off the trees and their realms on his fingertips. "Heaven, Hell, Earth, and Purgatory."

"What's inside the pods?" I ask.

"Golden energy. Firmament magic. Liquid power. That's what rejuvenates everything."

I hug my elbows. So many questions fly through my mind, I don't know where to begin. "How do I find the seedpods?"

Alden shrugs. "Oh, I'll help you."

"That's rather vague," says Tempest.

"There's a sphere we use. You ask it where the next seedpod is and it shows you. I've got it somewhere safe."

"It's Portia's now. It's safest with her, don't you think?"

"Sure," says Alden slowly. He turns his palm upward and whispers a quick spell. A small wicker sphere materializes in his hand. "This is it, see?"

"I do. Now, give it to Portia," says Tempest.

A long pause follows. A little too long for comfort. Why is Alden stalling about handing it over? I reach out to him. "I'll take that, thanks."

"You sure?"

"Positive."

Alden hands me the sphere. "Sure. Whatever. So, are we leaving now?"

Tempest rounds on me. "I need to talk to you alone, first."

Alden frowns. "Do you have to? It's critical we leave right away."

The fact that Alden doesn't want me talking to Tempest? It only makes me want to have the conversation more. "Actually, we absolutely need to talk now. Will you excuse us, Alden?"

"I don't like it, but it's your quest." Alden stomps off into the trees.

Once Alden is out of earshot, I focus on Tempest. "What's going on?"

Tempest sighs, like he knows what he's about to say is downright crazy. "Do you know the angel Verus?"

"The oracle angel? Sure. She had a prophecy for my parents." My brows furrow with confusion. *Not sure where he's going with this.*

"She asked me to be your Gatherer." Tempest sighs. "I know this will sound barking mad. Just hear me out." Tempest scrubs his palms over his face. "Verus said that you and I can save the Firmament. However, we have to do it in a very specific way. I must become your Gatherer. And the two of us must complete the quest alone."

A chill moves across my skin. Alone? Alden's the only one who knows what to do. "Anything else?"

"Unfortunately, yes. Best for last, luv. Before we open the final seedpod, we must go to Furonium. There's a special room that you need to visit. And you must wear a formal dress. Those are her instructions."

"Wow." Ball gowns. Special rooms. Oracle angels. Tempest doesn't look unbalanced, but that's a whole lot of crazy. And I have the after-realms to save. There's no room for distractions.

Alden pops out from behind the trees. "Well, now. Ready to go?"

My gaze shifts between the two men. It kills me to say this, but I have to put my responsibilities first. "Yes, I'm ready. Thanks for everything, Tempest. I think it's best if I go with Alden."

Tempest's gaze turns pleading. "Don't do this, Portia."

My heart clenches. This feels wrong. I remember Tempest carrying me away from the ruined Hearth. His presence calms me. It's like we've known each other for years. That doesn't make any sense. Still, it doesn't make the reality of the feeling any less. I press my palms against my eyes, like I can squeeze a good decision out of my head. "This is so hard."

"That's enough," says Alden. "We're done wasting time." He lunges forward, grips my wrist, and whispers a quick incantation. The world around me disappears.

Chapter Nine

The next thing I know, I stand in a darkened graveyard. The ground is covered with tombstones and fog. Shock and anger pulse through every nerve ending in my body. I did *not* say it was okay to take me here.

Alden stands a few feet away, his complexion pale with worry. "Sorry about that transfer spell. We couldn't waste any more time."

"Waste time?" My voice drips with anger. "You kidnapped me, Alden."

His voice quivers with regret. "I'm so sorry. I just needed to get us started."

Every inch of this guy looks miserable. My heart softens a little. It's not okay to go around kidnapping people. Although with so much on the line, I suppose that anyone can lose it. And all Alden's really wanted to do is start the quest.

I scan the rolling countryside. "Why did you bring me here? Is this where the first seedpod is?"

"No, there's something else we need to do. Every quest starts off with a small ceremony at this graveyard."

I shake my head. Quest ceremonies and abductions? Really? Alden's acting just as crazy as Tempest. "What's this ceremony for, exactly?"

"It's for you, Portia. I'll give you some magical energy and help you get started on your way. It's for your own safety."

"You'll give me magical energy?" My eyes narrow with suspicion. "I thought you said you were drained after your quest."

Alden sighs. "I've got a little in reserve, just in case. I know you're angry with me, but we need the ceremony. You need that energy. I don't trust your Gatherer. What is he, your ex-boyfriend?"

"No, I hardly know him." Even as the words leave my lips, I know that's a lie. Something about Tempest has always felt familiar.

"Well, whoever he is, he won't be at the ceremony."

A low roar breaks the quiet. My pulse kicks up speed. That sounds a lot like a dragon. "You might be wrong on that one."

"What?" The roar sounds again. "Is that the guy?"

"It's a safe bet."

"And he's a damned dragon? How could he follow us? I thought most of them didn't know magic."

In a weird way, I'm glad that Alden is quite possibly the only other person in the after-realms who doesn't know who Tempest is. "He's a wizard."

"Must be a pretty good one, if he can track my spells."

"He's the Emperor of the Furor. Greater demons have all sorts of abilities."

"What?" Alden's blue eyes stretch wide with alarm. "Damn!" He grabs my sleeve and starts dragging me into the mist. "We've got to hustle."

I pull my coat free. "Not until you tell me what this ceremony is about."

Alden's mouth trembles. "Millions of people are depending on us. You can't second-guess every little thing I do. Have you forgotten? I finished my quest. I had a Gatherer train me for it, too. You need to get with the program, and that means holding this ceremony. Am I making myself clear?"

Cold fingers of dread creep down my spine. The longer I spend with this guy, the higher the creep factor gets. "I'm not going anywhere with you."

A breeze kicks up around us, clearing away the mist. A dark shape blocks out the sky. It's a dragon with a sleek, black body, stout legs, broad chest, and a tail that's lined with spikes. There's no mistaking the sharp features, large eyes, and long scar by the jawline. Excitement and relief battle it out inside my chest.

Tempest is here.

He came for me. Sure, both Tempest and Alden have some crazy ideas. But one of them abducted me while the other flew to my rescue. As choices go, this one's looking pretty clear. I'm flying away with the dragon.

"You're leaving with him, aren't you?" Alden's shoulders slump. "Don't go. You need that ceremony, Portia. You need me."

Do I?

The weight of the decision presses in around me. Alden says I need his help and this ceremony. Tempest tells me to follow the guidance of Verus, even though her plan sounds insane. I turn over both directions in my mind. Two facts become clear. First, Verus and her prophecies have crossed paths with my family before. She's always been right. And second, going with Alden feels too easy. I don't have the kind of life where someone swoops in and fixes everything perfectly. No, I'm the girl who gets the mysterious angel and oddball plan.

Alden grips his hands together tightly. "You have to give me another chance. I'm your best bet to live through this. Hell, I'm the best bet for everyone. Please don't go. For all of us."

I straighten my shoulders. "Thank you for your offer. My mind is made." Turning on my heel, I walk toward Tempest at double-speed.

Tempest ruffles his wings and shoots me a crooked smile. A sense of rightness settles into my soul. My decision is made, once and for all. I climb up Tempest's foreleg and swing onto his shoulders. "Hi, Tempest."

"You okay, Portia? Did he hurt you?"

"I'm fine." Alden keeps staring at me. Every line of his body seems to droop with sorrow. "Let's go."

Tempest beats his wings in a regular rhythm. We rise into the clouds. I run my fingers over his scales. They're warm and leathery to the touch. "Thanks for coming to get me."

"I'll always come for you, Portia."

My heart stutters in my chest. It's like I'm on the balcony again. My feelings for Tempest are too strong for me to sort through right now. The after-realms are more important. I slip the wicker sphere from the pocket of my duster.

Time to get my mind back into saving the after-realms.

I set the wicker sphere onto my palm. "Show me where to go first."

The thin lines reform in the shape of a twisted iron gate. I smile with recognition and relief.

"What'd you see?" asks Tempest.

"The Onyx Gates."

"We're off to Heaven, then." He angles his body in a new direction and pumps his wings with more speed. Every beat of his wings brings me closer to the first seedpod. Will Tempest and I be able to open this thing on our own? A shiver of fear twists down my spine. Did I make the right decision to turn Alden down?

I certainly hope so. The after-realms are depending on it.

Chapter Ten

Tempest and I stand before a set of towering black gates made from intricately twisted iron. The whole thing looks hopelessly run down and rusted. My forehead creases with worry. Something here feels off.

"Are you sure these are the Onyx Gates?" I ask. All around us, I can only see waist-deep clouds in every direction. Overhead, the sky's a single sheet of white light. "Pops has taken me to Heaven before. It was all white towers, crystal walls, and blue skies."

"It's like this, luv," says Tempest. "There are the nice bits in Hell, like Furonium, and then, there are the dodgy spots in Heaven." He nods toward the gates. "Like this right here."

Odd shadows shift in the clouds around our feet. This whole place gives me the creeps. "Have you ever been inside?"

"No, but I've heard about it. The gates enclose a dream catcher."

My lips form a silent 'o.' I've read about places like

this. Dreams get stuck in here. Nightmares, too.

He shoots me a wry smile. "Once we cross the Onyx gates, it won't take long for our old nightmares to find us."

I set the sphere onto my palms. The threads of wicker weave into the words 'The Library floor.' "I guess we need to find The Library, whatever that means."

The gates open with a long creak. Tempest and I step past the threshold and into the realm of a dream catcher. A red door appears in the mist. I look around. There's nothing but cloud for miles in every direction. We open the door and step inside.

It leads us to my bedroom in Purgatory. Another version of me—a dream-self—lies asleep in bed, tossing under the crisp, white sheets. A chill crawls over my skin.

Something is wrong here. Very wrong.

Leave this place now, Portia.

Turning on my heel, I look for the exit. There isn't one anymore. I check out the walls and pull back the curtains. All the windows and exits have disappeared. I bang the plaster with the palm of my hand. "Open up!"

Meanwhile, my dream-self twists from side to side, still trapped in her sleep.

I round on Tempest, my heart thudding so hard I can feel its beat in my throat. "I have to get out of here!"

Tempest steps to stand before me. He keeps his hands at waist level, palms forward, as if I'm a wild animal that could bolt any second.

"It doesn't work that way in a dream catcher. You

know this, luv."

I force myself to inhale a few calming breaths. *Think, Portia. Tempest is right.*

"Right," I say, forcing my breaths to slow. "We have to wait."

"That's correct." Tempest gestures toward my dream-self. "And don't talk to her unless you have to. We'll both watch for a new door to open."

My dream-self thrashes harder under the sheets. Icy fear twists through my stomach.

Danger, Portia. Run!

"I don't like this, Tempest."

"Have you dreamt this scene before?"

"Not that I remember."

All of a sudden, my dream-self sits bolt upright in bed. She clutches her elbows as her shoulders tremble.

"Who's there?" she asks.

"It's just me," I say. "Portia. You're asleep."

Bit by bit, my dream-self turns toward me. When I see her, alarm rattles up my spine. Her eyes are a gooey shade of black. Dark tears ooze down her trembling face. I know that transformation. Every cell in my body goes on alert. Now, I know what's happening in this nightmare.

I'm turning into the Void. My limbs shudder with fear.

My dream-self reaches forward blindly. "Whoever you are, I can't see you. What's happening?" She reaches forward, her fingertips groping the empty air. The nails slowly darken with ooze. As my dream-self moans in horror, her body mutates into more blackened sludge. She tries to pull herself out of the bed, but her gooey legs won't carry her weight.

Instead, she tumbles onto the floor, weeping in terror.

I rush to kneel by her side. "It's okay," I tell her. "It's only a dream." I pat her quickly blackening hair. My fingertips come away covered in foul ooze. "I won't let this happen to you."

In reply, my dream-self curls onto her side and wails. "I'm doomed to turn into a demon. There's no avoiding that fate when you're Marked."

My eyes sting with tears as my voice grows louder. "I'm fighting this. We're fighting this. You're not turning into the Void. None of this is real."

But even as the words leave my lips, I know that it's all a lie. There's no guarantee I can save the after-realms, let alone myself.

Before me, my dream-self gasps for breath. Her lips and teeth blacken as air gurgles thickly in her chest. I stare into her dark eyes as her body splatters into the floor and disappears like a raindrop striking the pavement.

It happened. Maybe it was only a dream; it took place all the same. I saw myself transform into a Void demon.

Sitting back, I stare at my hands. Dark ooze is still there, slowly seeping into my skin. Maybe it's always been part of me. One day, it will fully claim my soul and I'll become a nameless, mindless demon gnawing on the Firmament; that is, if there's any left to consume. I'll never get out of this alive. Who am I to think I can help the after-realms when I can't save myself?

Tempest kneels beside me. He tentatively extends his hand toward me. I know he what he wants, and part of me wants to hold his hand, too.

The ache in my chest intensifies, but this is all too much, too soon. Besides, I don't even know why he cares about me or this quest. I give him the barest shake of my head.

No, don't come any nearer.

Tempest nods and lowers his hands. His demeanor mixes patience with concern. "You all right, luv? Talk to me."

When I speak, my voice cracks with despair. "Many people get Marked, and none of them get free. Even if I save the after-realms, chances are, I'll still change into a demon. Why am I bothering to fight this?"

Tempest leans in closer. "Listen to me carefully," he says. "The world is filled with people who tell you things are impossible and to give up. But that's only because they've already given up on themselves. Now, I don't know what the future holds. I do know that you're brilliant, Portia."

Our gazes lock. Somehow, his mouth moved until it's only inches away from mine. I want to run my fingers along the square line of his jaw, run my palm across the scruff of his cheek. I want to touch his bare skin. A sense of excitement fills the air. Something else is there as well. There's that same patience that I first felt when meeting Tempest on the balcony. He's waiting for me to make the first move.

Maybe I will. Chances are, I'm just acting crazy by trying to stop whatever it is that's happening between us.

I start to move my hand forward when a loud wail echoes through the walls of my dream-penthouse. At first, I think it might be my dream-self again. I shake my head. It can't be me. That's a young boy screaming. Tempest's mouth thins to an angry line.

"Do you know who that is?" I ask.

"I do."

My pulse beats at double-speed. "What does it mean?" Please, don't let it mean that I have to confront another version of myself transforming into the Void. Not sure I can handle that right now.

"That it's my turn."

The wail sounds once more. Muscles twitch along Tempest's jaw. Heat and rage pour off his body. Turning, Tempest looks over his shoulder. Where a smooth stretch of wall once stood, there's now a heavy iron door set into the plasterboard. Dragon runes have been roughly carved into the metal surface. I can translate them easily. They say one simple word: Dungeon.

Tempest stands. "Wait here. I'll take care of this."

"Not a chance. I'm going with you."

"This is the dungeon where my father held me as a child. You know the story?"

I nod. "Maxon told me."

"This dream is a familiar one," continues Tempest. "Chimera will be in the dungeon with me as a lad. I'm never able to fight." A low growl sounds in his voice as he adds, "That won't happen this time. I'll fight him."

I rise to stand beside him. "Good."

Tempest scans me carefully. "So, what are you saying?"

"If anyone tries to hurt you, then I want a piece of them, too."

"You sound protective, Portia." A low growl

sounds in Tempest's chest. I like that growl. In fact, I like it way too much for my own good.

My cheeks flush red. "That's what friends do for each other, right? We have each other's backs."

"Right." He keeps staring at me with such intensity, it's like I'm the center of the universe. For someone like me, this much attention is intoxicating.

Time to move on.

I gesture toward the door. "Lead the way."

Stepping forward, Tempest grips the door's heavy iron handle and hauls on it with all his strength. Little by little, the door swings open, revealing a long and low hallway made of rough gray stone. More iron doors line the walls on either side, separated by burnt-down torches.

As Tempest and I step down the long passageway, grimy hands grasp at the small barred openings atop each metal door. Desperate voices plead for water, mercy, and even death. The stench of decay and sick assaults my senses.

"Follow me," murmurs Tempest. "Last cell on the right."

It takes only a few minutes to reach the last cell. The journey seems to last much longer. The suffering and stench of this dungeon is beyond anything I could have imagined. Nausea twists through my stomach.

We step through the prison door to enter Tempest's old cell.

Like in the dream of my penthouse bedroom, the prison cell door disappears the moment we pass through it. Once we're inside Tempest's old dungeon, we're trapped with no way to escape. And when I look around the cell, escape seems like a good idea.

A scrawny teenage boy cowers on the grimy stone floor. He's curled up onto his side, his eyes staring forward, unblinking. His skin is mottled with angry red marks. I've seen those before in medical books. They're acid burns.

A man looms over the boy's body. It's Chimera. The bottom half of Tempest's father is humanoid, wearing simple britches and tall boots. The rest of Chimera is covered in dragon scales. Three different serpent-style heads jut out of his chest. All of those snake-like eyes are now focused on Tempest and me.

My legs tremble with fear as everything I've read about the last Furor Emperor flips through my memory. Chimera has three heads, and each one carries a different kind of venom sac. The first holds poison, the second creates a paralytic, and the third shoots acid. My breath catches as I think about the frozen boy and Chimera's powers. Tempest's father shot paralytic at his own son. After that, Chimera dripped acid onto his boy's unmoving skin. I suck in a rasping, horrified breath. My poor Tempest. How could anyone do this to a child?

Chimera's heads all tilt in unison. "Are you lost?" they all ask in a hissing, sing-song voice. My skin crawls at the sound.

The grown Tempest balls his hands into angry fists. "Not at all," he growls.

The boy on the floor twitches. On reflex, I kneel at his side and start casting healing spells. Like always, the words get tied up on my tongue, but I'm able to see some of the terror seep out of his eyes, at least.

Chimera inhales a long breath and keeps staring

at the grown Tempest. "I know your scent. You're Firelord, like me." He sniffs again. "And you're close to my bloodline."

Tempest's features stay still as stone. "I'm your son."

"You're him?" He gestures to the paralyzed boy. "The one I call the little teapot? He's so fragile, he could be made of porcelain. Somehow, I never tire of breaking him, though." The trio of heads lets out a sinister laugh. "And that's you?"

My hands clench into angry fists. When I want on patrol before, I've always shied away from killing demons. But killing Chimera? That wouldn't be a problem.

"I'm Emperor now. And my name is Tempest."

"Bah, I don't believe it. The little teapot? Never."

It takes everything I have not to launch into this guy and kick him in the head. Tempest looks at me, his features bright with held-in rage. He shakes his head. It's the barest motion. I know the meaning, though.

I got this, Portia.

Tempest rounds on his father. "You were a sorry excuse for a dragon before you took the crown. Spineless and weak. Becoming Emperor changed you into a greater demon and a bully to boot."

Chimera's heads flick backward in surprise. "Who told you that?"

"Mum. You don't remember her, but she remembered you all right. Before your change, you barely had one head, let alone three."

Chimera's heads swivel, looking between the frozen boy and grown man. "It's not possible."

"Why is so hard to believe that I would change when I accepted my role as Emperor? All it takes is a few short words."

My gaze falls to the skinny boy lying immobile and terrified on the dungeon floor. That boy accepted his role as emperor, and then he became a greater demon. But instead of gaining extra heads like Chimera, Tempest will add body mass and magical powers. I shake my head in awe. No one would have thought this boy would become the man who stands beside me.

Chimera's many mouths frown at once. "So you're called Tempest now, is that it? Becoming a greater demon got some magic to you. Added a few pounds and inches, too. And now, you've come to fight your old man."

"Something like that."

I stand closer to Tempest and lift my chin defiantly. "He isn't here alone. Tempest has friends."

Chimera's heads chuckle darkly. "A friend? I'm quite sure that's all you are."

"Leave her out of this," growls Tempest.

"Then don't waste any more of my time, boy. Say your piece and go."

"I will. With relish. Know this. I've undone every act that you deemed important. There are no more blood purges. No more destroying Furorling in a race to create a world of purebred dragons."

Chimera points straight at me. My throat tightens with a mixture of fear and rage. "Is that why you bring this mouthy Furorling wench before me?" His heads sniff the air wildly. "Why, you haven't even claimed her! In my day, I'd have rutted her first and killed her second."

It takes everything I have not to gasp in shock and fear. Still, I'm somehow able to keep my head high. Whatever happens, I won't let this freak know that he got to me. Tempest deserves that from a friend.

"Your day is over." Tempest gestures around the room. "And these very dungeons where you tortured me? They now overflow with your old followers. Anyone who worshipped the extremes of lust and wrath has been locked up and left to rot."

"Lies!" Chimera's eyes now blaze red with demonic rage. "I'll live for a thousand years."

"Actually, my grandfather Xavier fights you at the Battle of the Gates. He knocks you of the sky and you fall into a hole in the ground called Charybdis. After that, you're trapped for five hundred years until my brother releases you. In case you're wondering."

"Her brother brings you to me, and you die at my hand."

Chimera's many eyes narrow. "Xavier, eh? So, you're keeping her close to fight your demonic side, is that it?"

Tempest's irises flash with demonic wrath. "I said to leave her out of this."

"So that *is* the truth." Chimera's heads let out a laughing hiss. "There's no woman that can save you, son. You're a greater demon now. That means you're doomed. You'll become like me in the end. No one can fight the demon within, not for long."

Tempest straightens his shoulders, and if I could give him a high five without ruining the mood, I certainly would.

"I can," says Tempest. "I have for five hundred

years."

"Eternity is a long time, boy. That's my blood in your veins, after all. You'll see things my way one day."

"That will never happen."

Chimera moves into a half-crouch and growls. Fast as a whip, he lunges at Tempest. Just as quickly, Tempest slams his fist into Chimera's chest and pulls out his heart. Chimera stumbles backward, staring at the gaping hole in his rib cage. For a moment, Chimera looks as if he'll somehow regroup and make another assault. Then his body liquefies and seeps into the floor, just like what happened to my dream-self a few minutes ago. Tempest kneels beside the prone body of his younger self. "Keep the faith, lad."

I soak in this image of the two Tempests. On the outside, they look so different. One is tall, broad-shouldered, and handsome. The other is malnourished and sickly. But both have an inner strength that I've quickly grown to care about. *The Tempest in the teapot.* No matter what Tempest looked like, I think I'd always grow to care about the man inside.

The boy's eyes flicker to meet Tempest's gaze for a moment. After that, the younger version of Tempest disappears as well. A heavy pause hangs in the air. New and invisible cords of understanding reach out between us. It's more than my realizing the man that's really inside Tempest. It's discovering that both of us have spent our lives as warriors. In our cases, we're fighting so we don't become some kind of horrific demon. Tempest doesn't want to turn into his father. For me, it's the Void.

Tempest turns to face me. A sad smile rounds his full mouth. "What a fancy pair of bookends we make, you and I."

"All we're missing is matching markings."

"No, we aren't."

My breath catches. "You're Marked as well?"

"Not in the way you think."

"Then, how?"

Tempest shakes his head. "Something for another day, perhaps." He gestures across the cell. "It's time to go."

Following his point, I see a new door has appeared in the wall. It's made of polished oak with an elaborate golden handle. An inscription is carved along the top. I step in for a closer look. It's written in an ancient angelic dialect.

"Can you translate it?" asks Tempest.

"Yes, it says The Library of the First Angels." My pulse speeds with excitement and fear. "We made it."

Tempest and I step through the door. The library is a round tower that stretches far above our heads. Every inch of wall is covered with books. Walkways and ladders connect the different levels. Old-fashioned lanterns hang here and there, casting an odd glow. The familiar smell of old paper fills the air.

The floor of the library is only one story down. That's where the wicker sphere said we'd find the first seedpod. Tempest and I scale down the network of ladders. My limbs tremble with excitement.

If I can open one of these seedpods, I might save the lives of millions.

My palms turn slick as I scale down the ladder rungs. My pulse is so strong, the beat flickers the veins in my throat.

Guess I’m about to find out.

Chapter Eleven

Tempest and I quickly reach the Library floor. The layout mirrors the upper levels: books, rolling ladders, and walkways. A large globe sits in the center of the wood floor. The thing is massive and the air around it feels charged with magic.

"If you were going to hide a seedpod on the library floor, where would you put it?"

Tempest hitches his thumb toward the globe.

"Yeah." My chest tightens with worry. "So would I."

"Come on, luv." Tempest takes my hand and together, we walk up to the globe. It's covered in a metal casing that's painted to look like Earth. I tilt my head to one side, wondering. I don't sense any Firmament energy coming from this thing at all.

I reach forward, pause, and turn to Tempest. "What do you think?"

"Be careful. Move slowly."

"Right."

Reaching forward, I rest the barest tips of my fingers against the globe. Big mistake. A tsunami of power rushes through my system. The globe's metal casing bursts apart. Shards tear through the walls and my battle gear. Shrapnel bites into my shoulder and it burns with pain. Blood drips down my arm.

The last of the outer shell falls away, revealing an orb of golden light. My fingers get pulled deeper inside it. Energy pulses out of the orb, shaking the library to its foundation. The waves of power grow stronger. One slams into Tempest, sending him flying against the far wall. He sits like a rag doll, his head slumped on his chest.

Panic clouds my brain. Was Tempest knocked out cold? Is he dead? I try to move toward him. I can't, though. My hand stays trapped in the glowing sphere.

"Tempest! Tempest!"

He doesn't move.

Around me, the entire library vibrates ominously. Rolling ladders shift from side to side, their metal wheels creaking. Books shimmy and tumble from their shelves. The wooden slats beneath my feet curl and sway. A heavy sense of dread fills the air.

A second later, the place explodes.

Walls, books, and ladders fly off into empty space. I find myself in a disembodied cloud in Heaven. The sphere of power goes out of control. All my years of research on the Void and Firmament come down to this moment. What do I do next?

My brain spins through facts and options. This is concentrated Firmament energy. It's meant to rejuvenate the Scared Trees. I have to get it back to the Grove. I pull my arm, trying to free it from the sphere. Blood from my new shoulder wound drips down my hand and onto the orb. My movements turn more frantic. I still can't get free.

More energy floods my consciousness and with it comes pain. Agony radiates out from my fingertips. Liquid energy weighs down my limbs and fills up my lungs. It bursts from my body, a golden current of sparkling light that coils up into rolling clouds above my head.

Think, Portia. There must be something you can do.

Through the pain, an idea forms. I can cast a spell. Maybe that will free both the energy and me. I try to say the words, but it's like speaking underwater. Everything is garbled beyond use. Bits of skin tear free form my hands. I don't have much time left. My heart cracks.

And if I go, so do the after-realms.

An incantation fills the air. My breath catches. It's Tempest, casting a spell of rejuvenation. His Furor magic—which is so structured and solid—moves across my skin. It heals me.

Soon, it does far more than that. Tempest's Furor magic combines with the wild energy of the Firmament. The two powers meld in me for the first time. Furor and Firmament. Structure and chaos. Solid and liquid. When they come together, something wonderful happens.

I regain control.

Tempest's firm magic gives structure to the liquid energy of the Firmament, channeling the random flood of energy into a fast-moving river of purpose.

The vortex of power slows down enough for

Tempest to get closer. His free arm winds around my waist. His voice rings in my ears as he chants a spell of strength in dragon tongue.

At last, the glowing orb slips free from my hand and begins a slow plummet toward the earth. The agony in my body lessens. Once the orb is gone, the Firmament magic disappears from me as well. I feel hollowed out and exhausted.

I grip the wicker sphere. "Where's the next seedpod?" The strands reform into a new shape. I'm too tired to understand what it means.

"Our next stop is Earth," says Tempest. "But we aren't going anywhere until you've rested. And properly, this time. More than just spells."

I'm about to tell him that there's no time for stuff like that when my world fades into total darkness.

Chapter Twelve

When I open my eyes again, I'm safely tucked into bed at my Purgatory penthouse. Gray morning light glows from behind my sheer bedroom curtains. I peep under my covers and find that I'm in boyshorts and a loose T-shirt. I frown with confusion.

I don't remember getting ready for bed last night. I shake my head. Actually, I don't remember anything about last night after we opened the seedpod.

The seedpod.

Damn, the after-realms are falling apart. Why am I lounging around in my penthouse, exactly?

My bedroom door swings open. Tempest stands framed in the threshold. He's still wearing his black cargo pants, dark turtleneck, and kickass boots. He's dressed for battle and I look ready for a nap.

"Morning, luv."

I whip off my covers, march to stand before him, and set my fists on my hips. I do my best to look tough as I crane my neck to look up at him. "How long have I been asleep?"

"Enough, evidently." A smug smile rounds Tempest's mouth. "I consider this a success."

"That wasn't an answer." It's getting hard to keep playing tough, especially with those damned dimples of his. "I'm waiting." I try to sound angry, but the word comes out more as a question.

"Long enough to heal. And Doctor Tempest needs to examine your shoulder."

My eyes widen with surprise. "You do?"

"You were injured there, Portia. I need to check it before we go."

Without realizing I'm doing it, I tilt my head, giving him better access to my neck. His fingers brush my bare skin, and the feeling is divine. He pulls the neck of my T-shirt away with his left hand. The fingertips of his right hand smooth across my bare skin. A girl could get used to having Doctor Tempest around.

"You're going to have a scar, I'm afraid."

"Hey, I'm alive and ready to go back to work. Thanks for healing me."

Our gazes lock. This beautiful man spent all night fussing over me. If the world weren't about to end, I think I might kiss him. My timing sucks.

"Yes, back to work, luv." Tempest takes a pointed step away, breaking the moment. "You better get ready now. Your fighting suit is on the chair by your dresser. As is the wicker sphere."

"Yes. Fighting Suit. Dresser. Sphere." The way I say the words, it's obvious that I'm not thinking about any of those things.

"I'll wait for you outside." Tempest slips out the

door.

Once Tempest is gone, I get into my fighting suit with ninja speed. The sphere has just shown me the location of the next seedpod when the floor convulses beneath my feet. Pictures shatter. Walls crack. I brace myself against my dresser as Tempest runs into my bedroom.

"Another sinkhole," I say breathlessly. "We need to get out of here."

"The roof," he says Tempest. "That's the fastest way."

Hand in hand, we race out of the penthouse and onto the roof. Beneath us, the building rocks more violently than ever before. Tempest's body shimmers with white light as he changes form. Soon, he's a massive black dragon again. I scramble onto his shoulders and we quickly rise toward the clouds.

Below us, the world turns silent once again. The earthquake has stopped. My penthouse now stoops at an odd angle, its foundation busted. Car horns bleat in the morning air. Puffs of gray smoke rise from the nearby buildings. The welcome whine of police and fire trucks adds into the mix. My pulse skyrockets. What if some quasis were hurt?

"It's over," I say. "You can let me down. I need to check for any injured."

"Not yet," counters Tempest. He cocks his head and stares off toward the horizon.

"What's going on?" I ask.

"The earthquake hasn't stopped; it's just moved." Tempest points to the northwest with a graceful swoop of his neck. "It's going in that direction."

"Let's check it out."

Tempest and I fly over the metro district. Great slices open in the streets below us. Sidewalks tear apart. Buildings shift on their foundations. Terrified screams rend the air. My heart sinks. This is the worst sinkhole yet.

We're running out of time.

Tempest ups his speed. Soon, the concrete buildings give way to green swamps as we head toward the wetlands of Purgatory. Marshes stretch out before us. The quasis here live in houses built on stilts. We pass one small wooden building where a family of three is huddled onto the roof. The mother clutches a baby against her chest. The father waves us down. Their long chameleon tails twitch nervously behind them.

I lean over Tempest's side and wave at them in return. "I'll get help!" I call. "Well fly back and alert the President."

"There isn't time for that," says Tempest. He shakes his head. "This whole area is about to go. I can scent it on the air."

About to go. I know what that means. Everything will tumble into the earth, lost in a giant sinkhole. There's no time to fly back. There is one thing I can do, through. "Swoop in closer. The parents are too heavy for me, but I can grab the baby."

My pulse skyrockets as I grab onto Tempest's neckscales with my left hand and reach out with my right. "Hand me the child!"

The father gasps. "You're Princess Portia. You're doomed to turn into a full-blooded demon."

"And you're crazy to boot." The mother presses the child closer to her chest. "We're not handing our baby over to you. We'll wait for the regular authorities." She looks around and shrugs. "We've had earthquakes before."

"Damned quasis," growls Tempest.

"We aren't giving up," I say. "Let's give it another try. Go in for another pass."

Tempest swoops down once more. My palms turn slick with sweat as I lean over farther than ever before. The family clings to each other on the roof, protecting their child between them.

"I'm not what you think," I shout. "And this whole place is going down. I can't grab you but you can give me your…"

A great boom rattles the air. Everything below me—the swamps, trees, and houses—plummets into the earth. The last I see of the family is the mother offering up her child. Then, they all disappear into darkness.

"We have to go after the baby!" I shout.

A light bursts within the cavern below. The family reappears at the edge of the sinkhole. Another figure is with them. I shake my head in wonder. It's Alden.

The family hugs Alden close. He doesn't seem to know they exist. His gaze stays glued on me.

"What's he doing here?" I ask.

"Nothing good," says Tempest.

Alden cups his hand by his mouth. "I'm sorry, Portia. I really am here to help."

I stare at him, dumbfounded. If he truly wants to help us, Alden could make a big difference. I'm pretty sure I blew up a whole chunk of Heaven back there. I'm sure Alden knows how to sidestep that kind of trouble.

"We better go," I say. Tempest arcs his wings and we change direction.

"Wait!" cries Alden. "I have information about your family!" calls Alden.

I turn so quickly, I almost fall off Tempest's shoulders. "Tempest, wait."

"Hold on, luv." He moves us so we hover closer to Alden.

"Go on," I say.

"Your family." Alden's face appears completely open and innocent. "I asked around. They went to stay at Maxon's castle. It's safe there."

"Oh." An awkward silence presses in around us. "Thank you."

Alden jams his hands in pockets. "I'm here if you need me, okay?"

"Got it. Bye, Alden."

Tempest flies away so quickly, you'd think we were in a race. I fight the urge to look back at Alden. I have a feeling he's watching us go.

"Where to?" asks Tempest.

"Atlantis. You know much about it?"

"I've been there a few times. You?"

"I've studied their magic." Atlantis is an odd colony at the sea's bottom. It's made up of human witches and wizards who lost their home to an ancient earthquake and then used magic to resettle at the bottom of the ocean. They're hard to reach, so few people visit. "Can you fly us underwater?"

Tempest arches his wings. We shift direction. "On our way."

I grip onto his neck more tightly. *Seedpod, here we come.*

Chapter Thirteen

The sun shines in a turquoise-blue sky as Tempest flies us over the Pacific Ocean. Seagulls caw and dive through nearby clouds. I rest my cheek against Tempest's neck and try to think of useful ways to pass the time… Without worrying myself into a frenzy over the after-realms.

Not sure I do a bang-up job.

As a child in Antrum, my brother and I would kill time in royal carriage rides by counting the number of house crests in the crowd. Today, I'm counting the number of dark whirlpools that appear in the ocean below. Each new and blackened swirl of water is the sign of a fresh sinkhole that's just opened in the seabed below. Every time I see one, fresh adrenaline and worry charge through my system.

Another darkened circle appears on the waves. For a few seconds, the water stays black and deadly still. Then, it spirals downward into a shadowy vortex that reaches straight through the bottom of the sea.

The roar of a waterfall fills the air. The gulls squawk with fear. I shiver.

Fourteen whirlpools so far. A knot of worry tightens my throat. The after-realms won't last much longer.

"Atlantis is below us," says Tempest. "I'm going to cast a breathing spell on myself while I find a safe spot to dive. You better cast one, too."

"Got it."

Instead of trying my typical word-based spell, I close my eyes and summon the liquid Firmament magic inside my soul. Now that I know how that energy feels, I can tap into it more easily. Within seconds, the incantation flows from my lips. I could shout for joy.

"Ready?" asks Tempest.

I hunker down against his scaled neck. "Let's dive."

Tempest angles his head toward the ocean and curls his great wings against his body. We start a speedy descent toward the sea. Wind howls in my ears and scrapes across my skin. The small whitecaps that I saw from the clouds become tall and angry waves.

"Hold on," calls Tempest. "Here we go!"

With a great splash, Tempest and I break through the surface of the ocean. The water that envelops me is so cold it's like a thousand needles pricking my skin. I grip Tempest's back more tightly. The warmth of his dragon's body radiates into my own. Tempest flicks his tail, speeding us toward the ocean floor. Water whooshes over my body. All sounds become muted in the heavy seawater. My lungs ache as they pull in chilly liquid instead of air.

Soon Tempest slows his furious pace. I lift my head slightly and get a look around. A tall wall of black volcanic rock looms before us, its surface pockmarked with tiny cave holes. Tempest swings his long neck from side to side, scoping out which entrance to take.

With a quick nod, Tempest darts forward into one of the larger entrances in the cliff side. We zigzag through the submerged passageways until we break through the surface in a snug cave.

Ah, back to breathing air again. You never realize how hard it is to pull water into your lungs until there's a spell that makes you do just that.

The tiny cavern is lined with stalactites and stalagmites. The long structures jut out from the ceiling and floor, reminding me of massive teeth. Between the sharp rocks, the cave walls are covered in phosphorescent green algae. Everything is lit with a dim emerald glow. I slide off Tempest's shoulders and onto the cave floor. With a burst of white light, he returns to his human form.

"Make the journey all right?" he asks.

"I'm fine. You?"

"All in a day's work." He scans the surrounding cave and frowns. "They should be here."

"Who?"

"The welcoming committee."

"You've been in Atlantis before, right?"

"It's not what you call a holiday spot, but yes, I had some business here with the Electrophus tribe. They're our water dwelling dragons."

"Makes sense." I take in another deep lungful of air. It feels so good to breathe normally again. "If I were a water dragon in trouble, I'd hide down here, too."

Tempest chuckles. "That was the idea, until I found them, anyway."

A perfect silence follows, the sound broken only by the eerie drop-drop of water from the stalactites onto the floor. An uneasy sensation creeps into my joints. I've lived half my life in underground caves in Antrum. You can't so much as sniffle without someone hearing it halfway across our network of caverns. Stone echoes and amplifies everything. So why is Atlantis so silent?

"Humans live here," I say. "Where are they?"

"I don't know." Tempest's full mouth thins to a frown. "I don't like it."

With his left hand, Tempest gestures toward the exit tunnel. With his right, he sets his pointer finger over his lips in a 'shh' motion.

I nod, understanding what he wants. We're heading into Atlantis proper and need to stay silent. My heart decides that now is the time to start beating fast as a snare drum and twice as loud.

Tempest's tail arches over his shoulder, ready to strike. His shoulders square off. That's a fighting stance. I do my best to get battle-ready as well. I pat the thigh holders of my fighting suit and pull out my dagger. I don't really know what to do with this thing other than making a random stabbing motion, but my enemies won't know that.

Together, Tempest and I steal down the narrow exit passageway. Green algae on the ceiling casts a freakish glow over the scene. After a just few yards, we make a gruesome discovery: human bodies lie strewn on the passage floor. The Atlanteans are small with extra-pale skin and huge pointed ears like a bat's. They all wear Greek-style togas that are soaked with blood.

All of them are dead.

Great gashes have been torn through the bodies. Others have been partially smashed to a pulp against the cave walls. Every last one is marked with foul-smelling black ooze. My stomach churns with nausea.

The Void killed them. No question about it.

My body trembles with an overwhelming mixture of terror, rage, and grief. I don't know how I'll do it, but those demons will pay for this.

The dark corridor opens to a large underground cavern whose walls are covered in more glowing algae. Long strands of seaweed dangle from the cave's ceiling. Across the floor, the space is filled with a warren of streets and small, one-story houses made from loosely packed blocks of stone. Everything is quiet.

Tempest and I step out of the cramped tunnel and into the tiny streets. The copper scent of blood grows stronger. More bodies are strewn everywhere. The cobblestones are sticky with blood and black ooze. I grip my dagger more tightly. The blade wobbles in my grasp. I force my breaths to slow against the onslaught of terror. I feel a thousand eyes staring at me from the shadows.

Focus, Portia. Remember the seedpod.

I scan the stone buildings around us. In the center of the city, the columns of a circular Greek temple rise above the rooftops. A jolt of excitement tightens my torso.

That's a circular space. The Library floor was circular as well, and that's where the first seedpod was stored. Tempest and I share a knowing look. We don't need to say a word to know what we're both thinking.

The seedpod is in that temple.

With renewed speed, Tempest and I navigate through the twisting streets. The snick of our footsteps echoes through the quiet. An anxiety headache constricts across my temples.

Tempest and I quickly reach our goal: a small round temple. A large circular stone sits on the temple floor. My breath catches.

That's it. The seedpod.

All over the temple are signs that the Void ravaged this place. Black ooze drips everywhere: down the steps, along the columns, and especially on the round rock that sits at the temple's center. Deep gashes are cut into the stone with what look like claws.

The Void rampaged this temple, tried to open the seedpod, and totally failed. My guess is they're still nearby, waiting for me to open the seedpod for them. My skin breaks out in a thin sheen of nervous sweat.

Tempest looks to me and I meet his gaze. His eyes are filled with grim resolve. That same sense of determination solidifies in my soul, as well. I take care to lower my voice to a barely audible whisper. "I have to open that thing."

Tempest nods. "The stairs are the only access point to the temple." He keeps his voice quiet, too. "I'll keep watch. You release the seedpod."

It's a solid plan. Even so, my body feels weighted down with dread. Last time, I barely touched the golden energy inside the seedpod, and I almost killed myself while taking down a huge chunk of Heaven. The only thing that stopped me was when Tempest and I combined our magic. I bite my thumbnail anxiously. I was really hoping that Tempest could stand beside me when I opened this seedpod. That way, things wouldn't get out of control.

I scan the cramped stone city. The emerald light from the algae casts odd-shaped shadows onto the tiny streets. The dead bodies seem to stare at me plaintively, urging me to run while I still can.

But I won't run. And my only chance to open that seedpod is for Tempest to guard the quickest route of access to the Temple. I inhale a shaky breath.

You can do this, Portia.

I steel my shoulders. "Let's do this."

"One minute," whispers Tempest. "I need to get ready."

I nod and sheathe my dagger into its holster. That won't help me open the seedpod, anyway.

Tempest closes his eyes. Black scales appear on his skin in a wave that moves up from his throat and then rises across his face. When Tempest opens his eyes again, they're bright red with reptilian slits for pupils. He inhales a deep breath. Firelight glows behind the dragon scales in his neck. He mouths one word: *Go.*

I sprint up the temple steps, my boots slipping on the black goo that covers the ancient stone. As I close in on the seedpod, the cavern fills with a chorus of low, gurgling moans. A shiver of fear twists down my spine. No question who's decided to make an appearance. The Void.

I pause before the round stone that's set in the

center of the temple floor. Bit by bit, I lower my hands, stopping when my palms hover a few inches above the surface of the rock. Closing my eyes, I call to the Firmament power inside the stone.

Please let me be able to open this thing without touching it.

No energy answers my call.

I squeeze my eyelids more tightly shut and focus on the Firmament power with every fiber of my being. I find nothing. Disappointment crushes in around my body. I was able to contact the Firmament energy so easily when I cast the breathing spell. It's like the seedpod wants me to touch it. Craves me to become one with it and go out of control.

There's no way around this. The seedpod needs my touch in order to open. I glance over at Tempest. He still stands at alert at the foot of the temple stairs. His gaze meets mine and his irises flare with red light. He nods at me once. I know what the gesture means.

Do this, Portia.

Little by little, I lower my hands until my palms touch the round stone. The surface is cool and slick. A torrent of power speeds up my arms and floods my body. Within seconds, the stone shatters under my palms, revealing the golden sphere beneath. I try to step away quickly. No way do I want to get caught touching that golden energy directly again.

Try as I might, I can't move a muscle. Like a magnet, the glowing orb drags my palms deep into its gelatinous body. More Firmament power careens through me than ever before. Every cell in my body vibrates with energy. It's like my body's about to fly apart, bursting into a million pieces.

At that moment, hundreds of Void demons ooze out from the shadows in the darkened city. Even more appear within the dangling strands of seaweed that sway from the cavern's ceiling. One steps out of the crowd, its eyeholes glowing with red fire.

The Scintillion.

More power moves through me. I struggle to step away, but it's useless. Pain explodes inside my skull, making it hard for me to focus. Even so, I can make out the Scintillion in the eerie green light below. It steps forward.

Tempest tilts back his head, spouting an arc of fire toward the cavern ceiling. If he wants a show of power to make folks afraid, I can vouch that it worked on me. Once he's done, he refocuses on the Scintillion. "Leave now and you'll live," he warns.

The demon's gaping hole of a mouth starts to speak in its gurgling drawl. "You must see that you're out-numbered. I've a counter-offer. All I want is the Marked. Just leave her and go."

"Not bloody likely." Tempest exhales a jet of fire straight into our attackers. Dozens of Void demons burst into flames. Their bodies quickly dry out into husks of ash. The Scintillion is unharmed. Raising its arms, the Scintillion moves to strike Tempest.

Panic speeds through my nervous system. I have to help Tempest. Fire is his greatest weapon against the Void, and it won't work on the Scintillion. Why? I store that thought away to consider later. Right now, I need to break away from the golden orb. Digging in my heels, I pull backward with more force. The effort does no good. My hands stay locked onto the glowing surface of the sphere. More energy zings down my spine. The force is so great, it feels like every bone in my body is shattering. One thought echoes through my mind, over and over.

Must break free.

The power whirls inside me and around me. My surroundings turn dreamlike and hazy. I'm aware of Tempest fighting dozens of Void demons at once while pummeling the Scintillion with his bare fists. His clothing quickly becomes slashed and drips with ooze. Every part of my soul wants to run and help him, but I can't move from the spot. I can't stop the onslaught of Firmament power.

I have to get out. Out.

The last thought has such force that it combines with the Firmament energy. My wish merges with the power of the golden orb. Without meaning to, I cast a new spell.

OUT.

Firmament power does what my spell commands. I gasp as long, liquid arms of golden energy stream out of the sphere and whip around the temple. The sinewy strips ricochet off the stone houses. Golden streams slam into the cavern walls. Void demons are vaporized in their path. I strain to find any sign of either Tempest or the Scintillion. I can't find either.

A sense of foreboding chills me to the core. Did I just destroy Tempest along with the Scintillion?

There's no time to wonder. The golden arms pound the cavern walls in blazing, destructive arcs. Great chunks of seaweed tumble to the floor. A spider web of cracks appears in the glowing green algae on the walls. Fresh panic mixes with my steady pain.

The power of the golden orb is out of control.

Deafening cracks snap through the air. The cavern walls buckle and weaken. The arms of power keep pummeling the stone. Once again, I try to yank my hands out of the golden orb. I stay stuck.

An entire wall of the cave explodes. Rock blasts outward into the ocean beyond the cavern. The golden arms of power multiply and go berserk, pummeling everything in sight. A great wall of icy seawater slams through the newly opened wall. I can only watch in horror as a dark cliff of water churns toward me.

My body is swept up in the rush of freezing sea. My hands stay trapped within the golden orb. I can only focus on one thought.

Tempest.

More Firmament energy enters into my soul. The liquid magic swirls through my limbs. Agony slams into me. I feel like I'm being torn apart from the inside out.

I push my mind past the pain.

Tempest.

Water surrounds me. There's no time or breath left to cast a new breathing spell. I press my lips closed tight, trying to buy time before I drown. My body aches for oxygen. The golden arms of Firmament power whip around me, slamming into the submerged buildings. Great boulders and knots of seaweed twist through the ocean currents that now swirl around my body. My vision starts fade. My chest aches for air. I'm losing consciousness.

Out, out, out.

I've barely the energy for one last thought.

Tempest, please.

The pain in my body turns unbearable. My consciousness dissolves into the power of the Firmament. This is death, pure and simple.

A small voice sounds in the back of my mind. It's rolling, hypnotic and speaks in dragon tongue. I can't translate much of the spell, but that one word repeats again. *Rhana.* I suck in a lungful of seawater and can breathe it like air.

Someone's cast a spell on me. It's Tempest.

With the ability to breathe comes the capacity to feel pain once again. My hands burn where they touch the golden orb. Firmament power moves through me so quickly, it shreds my nerve endings with hurt. My mind rails against the agony.

Tempest's voice grows louder. The structure of his magic presses in around the wild, liquid energy of the Firmament. The arms of power twist and writhe as they wind into the glowing orb. I become aware of Tempest's warm body pressing into my back. He's behind me. He's alive.

We need to get out of here.

Gritting my teeth, I kick through the chilly seawater. With all the energy I have left, I try to free my hands once last time. Tempest's arms wrap my waist. His magic envelops my own.

My hands break free at last.

I crumple forward, my body suddenly feeling empty and lifeless. Tempest curls me into his arms. Together, we watch the golden orb settle down into the ground. I exhale with relief. I start to sob, the sounds muffled by the water that I now breathe for air.

We did it.

The golden sphere for Earth has been released. Just like the seedpod for Heaven, this one has returned to the Grove. There, it will rejuvenate the Firmament tree for Earth.

That happy thought is swept away as more ice-cold water pummels me. Tempest changes into his dragon shape. Dead bodies of Atlanteans float by, their faces now blue with death. A heartbeat later, Tempest has my coattails in his teeth. He yanks me through the water and sets me onto his shoulders. I loop my arms around his neck with all the strength I can muster. The fire inside him glows in the dark ocean currents as Tempest speed-swims toward the open ocean.

Tempest propels us forward. Huge boulders fall through the submerged cavern, the massive forms tumbling into our path. Tempest's tail swipes from side to side as he steers us around the debris of Atlantis and back toward the ocean proper. I'm vaguely aware of leaving the crumbling caverns behind and hitting open water.

I don't know how long we spend underwater It could be minutes. Could be hours. Eventually, we break through to the ocean's surface. The second we hit air, Tempest flips over and sets me on his dragon stomach. His reptilian irises look at me with concern. "That was more power than you wielded last time, and I thought last time was too much."

"Hey, I made it. Thanks to you."

"We make a good team." A soft smile stretches along Tempest's great dragon mouth.

My throat tightens with an emotion. Is it friendship? Something more? I shake my head, surprised by the intensity of my own feeling. Whatever it is, I decide that now's a good time to change the subject. The last few hours have been extreme enough without contemplating my relationship with Tempest. "What happened to the Scintillion?"

"Escaped," says Tempest. His lips curl up to reveal blade-like incisors. Clearly, he's not too happy that fact.

Every inch of my body aches. My eyelids start to flutter shut, but I'm able to push past the need for sleep. I pull out the wicker sphere and cup it in my palms. The strands quickly reform into a dragon. I smile weakly. "The next seedpod is in Furonium." The strands align into a new block-like shape. "Looks like a building."

"I know the spot," says Tempest. "Get you there in a jiff."

My hands feel numb as I jam the sphere into my pocket. "Good, we can't waste any time. We have to open those last two seedpods."

Tempest's dragon-face hardens into a worried frown. "You're resting first."

And let innocent people die? Not happening.

"That's what you say."

"Well, I am the Emperor."

I try to look badass. That's hard to pull off when I can't keep my eyes open. "And *I'm* the Princess."

"Clearly." He tilts his great head to one side and scans me carefully. I haven't known Tempest long, but I know one thing. He's plotting something.

"I won't change my mind on this."

"We'll be off to Furonium, then."

“You’ve got a scheme.” I blink sleepily, trying to figure out what he’s up to. “I won’t fall asleep on the flight over, either.”

“Wouldn’t dream of it, luv. Shall we?”

Without waiting for a reply, Tempest slides me onto his back once more. His great wings unfurl and flap across the water, causing the ocean’s surface to roil with the force of his power. Together, we take to the skies.

As we fly along, I use every trick I can think of to stay awake. No way am I letting him tuck me into bed like he did last time. To stay alert, I pinch my legs, pull on my ears, and even sing a few bawdy songs. Tempest appreciates the last tactic especially. His great rumbling chuckles fill the air.

An hour goes by before we land on a wide balcony. The building is a modern-looking two-story house that’s set into a cliff wall and overlooks a canyon formed from red rock.

We’re here. Furonium. At last.

Chapter Fourteen

Once we're safely landed, I slide off Tempest's back. The night air is chilly and bracing. I hop from foot to foot, trying to wake myself up. I'm so sleepy and out of it, I almost fall on my butt. Guess even a tiny bit of motion is too much for me right now. I am bone tired. Maybe I can ask Tempest for a cup of coffee before we head out again.

Across the balcony, Tempest returns to his human form. Once the transformation is complete, I can't help noticing how his clothes are little more than rags. Fresh red scars peek out from under the long tears in the fabric. Guilt and sympathy battle it out in my heart.

"You got hurt," I say slowly.

Tempest shrugs. "Dragons heal quickly."

"We should get you some first aid or something."

"No, we should talk about getting you some proper rest."

"Tempest, the after-realms are falling apart. The

Scintillion is out there. That crazy guy Alden is either actually a nice person or a somewhat creepy stalker."

"More like a wanker, I'd say."

"With all this going on, you can't talk me into resting." The word 'resting' makes me want to yawn. I do an awesome job of not giving into the urge.

"How about a compromise?"

"I'm listening."

"One mo." Tempest steps inside what I can only assume is his house. A minute later, he returns holding two thick cotton robes and an opened bottle of wine. "You're in wet clothes and need a quick rest." He raises the robes on his right arm. "This is for the clothes." He lifts the wine in his left hand. "This will help you rest."

I huff out a tired breath. Tempest is wearing me down on this. Those robes look mighty comfortable, too. "All right, bring it here."

"You won't regret this." Tempest hands me the opened bottle. I quickly scan the label.

"Oh, hey," I say brightly. "I've heard about this stuff. It's angelflower wine. Maxon says it's awesome." I press the bottle to my lips.

"Hold on there, luv."

By the time the words have left his mouth, I've already enjoyed a few deep chugs of the yummiest wine ever. I'm not much of a drinker. This stuff is super tasty, though. I down a few more swallows because it's just that good. After that, I smack my lips and lower the bottle.

"What's that you said?" I ask.

"I was about to say to only take a small sip." Tempest shakes his head. "That's rather strong stuff.

One sip makes you sleepy, but more than that—"

"Hey, wait a second." For some reason, Tempest starts wobbling from foot to foot. I set my hand on his upper arm. "Stop swaying around."

"I'm not," he says with a sigh. "Angelflower wine acts quickly. In larger quantities, it makes you rather alert and squiffy."

"Naw, there's no squiff here. Don't feel a thing." The temperature spikes about twenty degrees. "Hey, what's up with the weather around here? Why's it so hot all of a sudden?"

"It isn't, Portia."

"Liar, liar, pantssafire." My mouth has a tough time getting words out correctly for some reason. Not that I care. It's been a long day and I'm celebrating. Besides, my clothes are way too suffocating to focus on the weather anymore. I toss my duster coat onto the balcony floor.

"What're you up to, luv?" There's a sexy growl in Tempest's voice that I like. A lot.

"These clothes are stifling." I quickly peel off my fitted top and chuck it onto the ground. After that, I shimmy my leather pants onto the floor. Ah, undies and a bra. Just the right amount of clothing. "Better, am I right?" I do a catwalk across the balcony.

"Bloody hell." Tempest pinches the bridge of his nose. "You do realize I'm the greater demon of lust, right?"

I panic. *He wouldn't say that if he liked my body, right?* "What? Do you think I'm ugly or something?"

"No. I think you're gorgeous, Portia."

"Knew it." A warm sense of satisfaction runs through my veins. Or maybe it's the wine. Either way,

I need another drink. Rising the bottle, I go for another gulp. Tempest snatches the wine away for himself. Greedy dragon.

Tempest tries to hand me a robe that looks so warm, it could be made of fur. "You need to put this on," he says.

I fold my arms under my chest. "You're not the Emperor of me."

"Portia. You've drunk enough angelflower wine for a legion of dragons. I think you should trust my judgment here."

"Fine." I swipe the robe from his hand, march across the balcony, and toss it over the side. "So there." It drifts slowly down to the canyon floor. I flip around to face Tempest. "And that's what I think of your robe."

He puffs out a breath. "Crikey."

"Don't be a drama Emperor. It's too hot out and you know it. Besides, you've got to be uncomfortable, too. Cut a girl some slack."

Tempest inspects me carefully. He's coming up with a new plan, I can tell. "All right, how about this? I take off my turtleneck so I can be comfortable."

"I like this idea."

"And then, you and me go inside where it's all nice and cool and put on robes. How's that sound?"

I purse my lips, interested. "You have a deal, my friend." My head gets all fuzzy again. "Maybe."

"Brilliant. Ladies first." Tempest approaches me with the second robe like it's a net and I'm a small forest creature in need of catching. It's the funniest thing I've ever seen. I laugh so hard, I double over.

"Just let me drape this—"

The moment the fabric touches my shoulders, I grab it ninja-fast and toss it over the balcony, just like the last one. In the canyon below us, someone makes an 'argh' noise. After that, a sound follows that's like glass crashing. Tempest leans over the railing. "Sorry about that, Reginald!" He turns around to face me. "You promised to wear the robe, Portia."

"I said maybe." An idea appears in my mind. *Why didn't I think of this before?* "Let's go inside and jump on your bed!"

"Jump." Tempest closes his eyes and groans like I'm making his life miserable or something. "On my bed."

"Yeah." I grab his hand and drag him toward the door. "Come on, you."

Tempest sighs and lets me drag him into his bachelor lair. What a sourpuss. Wait until he hears my amazing plans for after we jump on his bed. This is going to be the best night ever.

Chapter Fifteen

When I open my eyes again, I find myself in a modern bedroom decorated in shades of black, white, and red. Tall windows line the walls; a plush white rug covers the floor. I lie naked in a massive bed under black silk sheets. Tempest sits in a chair beside me.

Wait, what?

I sit upright and tuck the sheets under my arms.

Tempest's large brown eyes lock with mine. "Morning, luv." His long legs are kicked out before him with his biker boots crossed at the ankles. He wears a fresh pair of jeans and a stretchy black T-shirt. It's not fair how messy and sexy he looks in the morning.

"Hey." My voice comes out as a nervous chirp.

Smooth, Portia.

I pat my hair, finding a positive rat's nest of blonde tangles surrounding my head, halo-style. I open my mouth to ask questions. Instead, I put my foot straight into it. "This is a lot of me naked in your bed, Tempest."

He eyes me mischievously. "Do you always start conversations this way?"

My cheeks burn red with embarrassment. "How did I end up, you know?"

"Naked in my bed?"

I bite my lips together hard. *This is so humiliating.* "That part, yes."

"You don't remember?"

"No, should I?"

"Perhaps not. You were a little out of it after the angelflower wine."

"Oh, the wine." I lie in bed, close my eyes, and debate about casting a disappearing spell. "I got a little tipsy, I think."

"I'd say all-out blasted. You had lots of plans, including jumping on my bed."

"Did I?"

Kill me now.

"Oh, yes." A sneaky look returns to Tempest's expression. "I didn't join in the jumping bits myself, mind you. I must say I enjoyed the show, though."

My cheeks burn about eight shades of red. "What did I do after that?"

"Ah." He laces his fingers over his taught stomach. "You decided that we needed to sleep together. You were most adamant about doing so without clothing."

I'm so stunned, my eyes almost bug out of my head. "I said that?"

"You most certainly did." Tempest winks. "I was quite shocked."

"Did we…" I want to pull the sheets over my

head. I grip them more tightly instead. *Wow, do I ever feel like an ass.* "You know?"

"Have sex?"

I wince. "Yes, that."

Tempest chuckles. "Why, Princess Portia. I'm not that kind of dragon."

I kick at his boot with my bare foot. "I'm serious."

Tempest meets my gaze and the laughter disappears. "I could tell you weren't yourself, luv. I'd never take advantage of you like that. We negotiated."

"Thank Heaven."

"Don't give the angels any credit for what happened."

I can't help but chuckle. "Okay, thank *you*."

"Quite right. In the end, we decided that I could sleep in the chair beside your bed. You could then be naked and that was close enough to count."

I exhale a relieved breath and curl onto my side. "Thanks again."

"You've only been out for an hour or so. Time enough for me to cast some spells of healing and nourishment. A few whoppers to cover a hangover, too."

"I owe you." I want to say more; I can't find the words. It even gets hard to meet his gaze. Tempest is a special guy.

There, I said it. He's kind and caring. I'm so lucky to have him with me on this quest.

"Since you're in the mood to remember your debts, I have to remind you about the angel Verus. After we open the next seedpod, we have a quick stop we need to make."

My brows draw together with shock. Did I say

Tempest was kind and caring? I forgot about the odd Verus prophecy part, too. Not sure what to make of all that. Even less sure that I'll go along with it. Some things are too weird.

The room shudders with a wave of tremors. Fresh adrenaline pumps through me. We need to get back on our quest.

"How bad has it been?" I ask.

"We've been getting tremors like this for the last hour." The floor stops moving. "They don't last long, though."

I scan the room for my wicker sphere. "We need to get going." I grab the magical object and speak directly into it. "Where in Furonium is the third seedpod?" The sphere doesn't move. The long strands don't even twitch. I frown. "Do you think it's broken?"

"It's fine, luv. You already asked it last night. It stopped answering you after six times or so."

I groan with embarrassment. "Why am I not surprised? So, what did it tell us?"

"The third seedpod is in a storage cave that's not too far from here."

"Cool." Now that I'm rested and jacked up on healing spells, I feel ready to take on the world. I wrap the sheet around my torso and slide out of bed. "I'll be ready in ten minutes."

Chapter Sixteen

Tempest and I walk along the basin of a red stone canyon. The air is still and quiet. No one else is around. Striped rock walls rise on either side of us. A pale blue sky arches overhead. A bubbling stream meanders through the yellow scrub grass on the canyon floor. We've followed this slim waterway for more than an hour. Not far from here, it should pass the cave where the third seedpod's hidden. My heart lurches at the thought.

Only two seedpods left to go.

Small stones tumble down the canyon wall with a clickity-clack. My chest tightens with alarm. I twist around, scanning for trouble. Evil energy oozes out of the shadows.

"It's the Scintillion," I say in a low voice. "That monster's nearby."

Tempest scans the swirling rock formations. "I can sense it too."

I cup my hand by my mouth. "We know you're here and we're not afraid of you!" The word 'you' echoes for an extra-long time through the canyon. It sounds badass that way, which makes me feel a bit more confident, even if I don't really feel that way on the inside.

Tempest and I approach the mouth of a small cave. This is it. He pauses beside the darkened entrance. "We go in as a team. Safer that way."

"Sure." My voice comes out clipped and anxious.

Together, Tempest and I step inside. The cave is a long and low space. Corrugated metal boxes are stacked everywhere. Each one's marked with different magical ingredients. I scan the labels. Dried eye of newt. Elder dragon scales. Powdered reindeer horn.

"Is this Hexenwing storage?" I ask. If there's one Furor tribe I know something about, it's the Hexenwings. Outside of Tempest, they're the only ones who use magic.

Tempest strolls around the room, inhaling deeply. "Yes, but they haven't visited this place in years." He pauses. "Someone else has, though." Tempest's tail arches over his shoulder as his body goes into battle mode. An eerie sense of menace seeps out from the darkened corners of the cave.

A jolt of awareness skitters across my skin. This is exactly how I felt in Atlantis when I met the Scintillion.

"You can come out now," I say.

The Scintillion's gurgling voice creeps in from the shadows. "There's no need to worry. I'm not here to kill you."

Sure, you aren't.

A hulking silhouette steps out from behind a stack of crates. Although I've fought this monster many times, I've never gotten a good look at the thing. The Scintillion is tall and broad with a barrel chest and long arms. Blackened goo oozes off every inch of its body. The monster's fiery eyes focus right on me.

My chest tightens with dread. That thing wants me dead, there's no question about it. The stench of rotting flesh slams into me, making me sick to my stomach.

"I know the two of you are powerful," says the Scintillion. "You proved that in Atlantis. I'm here to make a deal."

Tempest moves, placing his body between the Scintillion and me. I grab the dagger from my thigh holster and hold onto it tightly. My hand shivers with nervous energy, and the blade taps lightly against my thigh.

"What kind of deal?" I ask.

The Scintillion steps closer, its movements making nasty slurping noises against the floor. Tempest raises his arm. "That's close enough." The monster pauses.

The Scintillion's long black tongue licks its thin lips. "This is my proposition. The Marked are rich with Firmament energy. I need just a little taste of that power. Give it to me and I'll hunt you no more."

"Bollocks," says Tempest. Dragon scales appear over his exposed skin. The scent of charcoal fills the air as he preps his lungs to breathe fire.

"My offer isn't for you," says the Scintillion. "What do you say, Marked?"

I tap my chin, considering. I haven't spent my life

poring over research only to ignore the facts now. They tumble through my brain, the information taking a new shape in my mind. A realization slowly seeps over me. I don't have to be afraid of the Scintillion. He should be afraid of me.

"Want to know what I think?" I ask. "You were telling the truth before. You didn't come here to kill us. You already tried that in Atlantis. Brought along an army, too. And you failed. So, you know you can't win in a head-on fight."

The Scintillion's eyes flare with fire. Warm satisfaction spreads through my chest. His silence says that I'm right. I feel like a shark that smells blood in the water. I'm going in for the kill.

"And now you're negotiating." I shake my head. "With what, exactly? Want to get your ass kicked again? Bring it on. Like hunting us across the after-realms? Be our guest. Only make no mistake. Get out of my way. I have seedpods to open and I swear, if you slow me down, I will kill you so dead you'll never ooze your way out of battle again."

The earth trembles. Tiny rocks careen down the cave walls. Metal boxes rattle against the floor. Somewhere, more sinkholes are opening up and doing damage. The thought makes my blood boil. "Want to know what scares me right now? Not you." I point at the cave wall. "That scares me. The after-realms falling apart. Are we clear?"

The Scintillion lets out a gurgling roar. Tar flicks off its body as it shudders with rage. For a moment, I think the thing's going to attack again. My body tenses, waiting for the blow. But that doesn't happen. The Scintillion collapses into a puddle on the rock floor and oozes away into the ground. I stare at the spot in disbelief.

He left. He really left. Guess I'm better at giving speeches than I thought.

My gaze stays locked on the cave floor. "Do you think we saw the last of him?"

Tempest steps up behind me. "No."

"Me neither." I turn around to face Tempest. "Let's get that see—"

Tempest's mouth is on mine in an instant. Our tongues meet. His hand fists my hair. I loop my arms around his neck and press myself against him, hard. It's the best feeling in the universe. It's over way too soon. Tempest breaks the kiss and presses his forehead to mine. We're both panting for breath, our arms still entwined.

"What…" It takes me a few seconds to organize my thoughts. "What was that for?"

"After that speech? I gad to give you a kiss. You're magnificent, Portia." Another jolt hits the cave floor. "But the after-realms? They're a bloody mess. We better go."

"Right." It's an effort to unwind my arms from him. "Time to find that seedpod."

There's an awkward moment where we're standing close and not doing anything about anything. The kiss replays in my mind. Unbelievable. Tempest and I are coming together while the after-realms are falling apart. That makes it official. My love life is actually a bad country-western song. If it weren't for bad luck, I'd have no luck at all.

Time to focus to the quest again.

"Where's the deepest part of this cave?' I ask. "I'm

guessing that's where the seedpod will be."

"That's the sub basement, two floors below us."

"Lead the way."

Tempest and I climb down a rough-hewn staircase. It looks clawed out of the rock by dragons. Maybe it was. We reach the sub-basement. Floor lights blink on in succession, revealing the space. What I see is a mess. The floor's jammed with random-looking piles of junk. There are open urns of powder, cracked chests of gemstones, and piles of dried-out herbs.

Closing my eyes, I reach out with my senses, searching for Firmament magic. The liquid power instantly rushes through my soul. "The seedpod is nearby, no question about it."

"Let's tidy up then." Tempest whispers a quick incantation in dragon tongue. His deep and rumbling voice echoes through the small space. Instantly, all the junk slides into neat piles along the walls, or arranges itself onto shelves.

With all the garbage out of the way, it's clear what to focus on next. A large, circular lump juts out of the center of the floor. My pulse quickens. This thing is about the same size as the other seedpods. I take a cautious step closer. The energy radiating from this spot is overwhelming. My hands turn slick with sweat.

I can't stop thinking about the seedpod in Atlantis. When I tapped into the Firmament's power there, I blew out the entire cavern. And before that, I wiped out the Library in Heaven. Not the best track record.

My knees tremble with worry. "I think we need a plan here."

Tempest moves to stand behind me. "Perhaps we team up again, only on purpose this time. Maybe we cast a spell of opening together?"

My shoulders slump with relief. "That's it. We'll cast the spell of opening first. After that, I'll touch the stone. No need for both of us to get stuck."

"Right." Tempest moves to stand behind me. His firm chest presses into my back. Bit by bit, he slides his hands down my outer arms, stopping when his fingers grip my wrists. "Have a preference for the incantation?"

I stare at our arms. The physical connection is comforting. "Dragon tongue. There's one that starts with the words 'karrah raz.' Do you know it?"

"Yes."

"Then let's begin in three, two, one."

We start casting together, our voices chanting in unison. The power of Tempest's magic surrounds me, strong as a mountain. My heart lightens.

Our magic has met before, but this time, it does something else. Combines. His firm Furor strength and my liquid Firmament power. Our casting builds off the abilities of the other. The spell takes on a new meaning and strength. It becomes its own entity, gains its own magical signature. Fluid yet strong. My stance firms with confidence. Our magic is entwined. Together, we can do this.

I set my hands onto the round stone. The words of our casting grow louder and more intense. The rock cracks beneath my fingers. Golden light shines through.

There's no need to speak. Both of us know what to do next. Moving as one, we pull our joined arms away from the glowing sphere of power. The movement is easy and smooth. The yellow orb of power sinks into the earth, just like all the others.

An odd memory appears in my mind: the canopic jar spell on my penthouse floor. How will these golden spheres help the Sacred Trees? A happy thought occurs to me. Soon I might see the answer to that question first hand.

"We did it," I say numbly. "The third seedpod."

"We're a good team." Tempest releases my arms and steps away. "Question is, what do we do now?"

I rub my neck in an anxious rhythm. "About that. Do we still need to do that trip Verus asked for?"

"That we do, luv."

I press my palms onto my eyes, like I can squeeze this reality out of my head. We were so connected while casting that spell. Now, we're back to crazy stuff like oracle angels. "Why does Verus want us to do this again?"

"Verus saw the Firmament fall apart. She tells us only what we need to know in order to stop that from happening. And right now, we need to dress and go to this chamber. I can't tell you why. I know it sounds daft." He steps in front of me, taking my hands in his. The touch is firm, warm, and electric. "But it's not crazy, luv. Trust me. The after-realms depend on it." Every line of his face is marked with intensity. "And it would mean the world to me, too."

Our gazes lock and a realization moves between us. We are a team. And in a team, you cover the other person's back, even if it seems crazy at the time. "Can we be done in an hour or two?" I ask.

"Less than that."

I give his hands an encouraging squeeze. “In that case, let’s get ready.”

Chapter Seventeen

Tempest and I stand before a blue stone castle topped with dozens of golden towers. The thing looks like it fell out of a fairy tale. Tempest swings open the fancy front gates and we step inside a large reception room. This space towers two stories high and is decorated with marble archways, blue murals, and golden accents.

"What do you think?" asks Tempest.

I turn around. My gown swishes across the marble floor with the movement. It feels strange to be out of my fighting suit. However, Verus said I needed to wear a gown, so a gown it is. For his part, Tempest wears his black combat pants with a Henley.

"This is lovely," I say. "Did you evict Cinderella to get it?"

"Not quite." Tempest chuckles and the sound warms my heart. "One of the Chieftains gifted it to me when I became Emperor. Now, I use it as a private retreat of sorts." He scans me from head to toe. The attention makes me blush. "You look beautiful, luv."

"Thanks." I shift my weight nervously from foot to foot. "When does this get started exactly?" I don't know what Verus has planned, but I'm ready for it to be over. Tempest and I already checked the wicker sphere. The last seedpod is at the Grove.

Tempest leans against the wall, his left biker boot hitched over his right. His eyes are glazed over.

"Tempest."

He shakes his head. "What?"

"Did you hear my question?"

"Missed it." He rakes his hand through his loose, black hair. "Apologies. I suppose I'm a bit distracted." He eyes me from head to toe again and smiles.

I tilt my head and wonder. *What's up with him, anyway?* "You act like you've never seen a girl in a ball gown before."

He folds his arms over his chest and chuckles softly. "Funny you should say that, as a matter of fact."

New sounds fill the reception hall. There's the lilt of a Viennese waltz, along with laughter, chatter, and the clinking of glasses.

I frown in confusion. "Sounds like someone's having a party."

"It's a formal ball." Tempest nods toward an archway at the far end of the reception room. "That's where you need to go."

My brows lift with surprise. "And you're not going with me?"

"Funny you should say that, too." The look on his face is unreadable. "Knock on the doors at the far end of the hall. That's all I can tell you."

"Right." I have a dozen questions I could ask, but I'm guessing Tempest can't answer them anyway. Ah, Verus and her visions. Oh, well. The sooner I finish whatever this is, the faster we can open that last seedpod. "Be right back."

I feel Tempest's eyes on me as I follow the hallway to a set of golden doors. Here the music and chatter grow louder. An electric sense of anxiety charges my bloodstream. I don't like formal balls, even when I know who's going to be there.

Stop stalling Portia. There are bigger things at risk.

Screwing up my courage, I knock on the door. It swings open to reveal a servant in a crisp tuxedo. His black hair is gelled over neatly to one side. "Good evening, Miss." His British accent is very proper.

I curtsey. "Good evening. I'm here for the ball."

The man spots my markings and frowns. "You weren't on the guest list, I'm afraid."

"Emperor Tempest invited me."

The servant steps backward and swings the door wide open. "Come in. You'll find his Imperial Majesty at the bar."

My brows lower with confusion. "That can't be right. I just left Tempest in the outer Hall."

The servant bows slightly at the waist. "Perhaps I was mistaken."

"That's fine. Thank you." I step inside the ballroom. Marble arches line the blue walls. A string orchestra plays in one corner. Furor nobility talk in small groups or waltz across the dance floor. The men all wear black tuxedos; the ladies are in gaudy gowns. I'm no fashionista, but those dresses went out of style twenty years ago.

What is this place?

I wander along the fringes of the crowd. I've never had a chance to watch the Furor, and their society is fascinating. So are their armscales. Many of the women wear sleeveless gowns to show them off. Men toss off their jackets and roll up one sleeve to display theirs. Couples have matching patterns, too. It's sweet. Before I know it, I've meandered my way to the bar. What I see makes me freeze in place.

He's here. Tempest.

Only it's not him. This version of Tempest has slicked-back hair and a smug grin. He's missing some of his scars, too. There's a full glass of whiskey in his left hand and a woman under his right arm. She's a dark-haired beauty with bright red lips. At least, she doesn't have a pattern to her armscales. They aren't a couple. My eyes widen with a realization.

They might not be from this time, either.

I scan the ballroom. All the make-up and hair looks decades out of style. And Tempest seems so different, too. Verus must have sent me back in time? Why?

Tempest downs his whiskey in one gulp before leaning over to nibble at the woman's neck. She moans with pleasure.

A sense of betrayal sears my heart. Tempest is acting exactly like the 'hit it and quit it' guy that Maxon warned me about. It's a younger version of Tempest, but still. A knot of sadness tightens in my throat.

A Furor man steps into my line of vision, blocking my view of Tempest. He's tall and slim with neat blond hair and a square jawline. A nest of scars winds up his neck.

"Good evening, Miss." The man's accent is British, clipped, and formal. Funny how the English can say the same words and have such different meanings. The servant's 'good evening' was deferential. This man thinks I'm pond scum.

"Good evening to you." I skip the curtsey this time around.

"You're thrax." The way he says the word 'thrax,' I can tell he's not a fan.

"Yes, I am."

"Your kind isn't welcome here."

I blink hard with disbelief. "Not welcome? Maxon was in line for the throne."

"You know that traitor? He just turned into an elemental and deserted us."

"Oh, that's right," I say carefully. "When did that happen again?"

A dragon's growl sounds in the man's chest. "Last month."

My mind races through what this means. Verus sent me twenty years into the past. But why? Without meaning to, I whisper under my breath. "Verus, what are you doing?"

"Are you a friend of Verus?" asks Mister Friendly.

"Not directly."

"Don't play word games here. That troublemaker came around last week, asking my Uncle questions."

I look him over from head to toe. A realization hits me. "You must be Epsilon." This man is Tempest's nephew. Maxon told me all about how he was abducted by rogue thrax hunters as a child. If it hadn't been for my father, Epsilon would have died.

Even so, the guy never forgave the thrax.

"Verus sent you didn't she?" A nervous twitch flickers by Epsilon's mouth. "Tempest told me she came round last week, asking him to become a Gatherer on some foolhardy quest. He refused outright and now, she's sending pretty thrax wenches in to plead her case." Silver light glistens around Epsilon's body as he changes into his dragon form. Compared to Tempest, he's a small beast. But what he lacks in size he more than makes up for in barely contained rage. When he speaks, his voice is a menacing snarl. "Tell Verus her little scheme is a failure."

I take a cautious step backward. "That's not what this is about."

Epsilon extends his wings and takes to the air. The crowd stills. Hundreds of eyes lock in our direction. My pulse skyrockets. "I said leave," snarls Epsilon. "Now!"

There's nothing like an angry dragon to send you off in a panic. And panic, I do. Turning on my heel, I run for my life in the opposite direction. I don't get too far before I hit a wall. Only it isn't a wall. I look up.

I ran straight into the younger Tempest. He's all smarmy smile and charm. "You'll have to forgive my nephew. He's not fond of the thrax."

I don't say anything. I can't. It takes everything I have to keep looking in this stranger's eyes, trying to find the Tempest I know. The man I love. There's no caring in this Tempest. No sympathy to his soul. Every inch of this man is a player. Compared to the Tempest I know, his is a hollow game.

Tempest waves his hand dismissively. "Excuse us, Epsilon."

"But Uncle, she's a spy sent by Verus."

Tempest keeps his gaze locked with mine as he speaks to Epsilon. "I'm more than capable of handling one thrax girl."

"Yes, Uncle." Epsilon returns to his human form and walks away.

"I'm sorry if he scared you," says Tempest. "Perhaps I can make it up." He starts working his crooked smile and something about it looks hollow. Instead of tempting me to grin back, it only makes feel lonelier. I miss my Tempest.

I stare out into the crowd. I can't hold a gaze that is Tempest and isn't, all at the same time. "I'm fine, thank you."

He steps closer. "What happened?"

"What do you mean?"

"There was a look in your eyes. It's gone now."

"Oh." I twist my fingers together nervously. "You remind me of someone I care about."

"That's one lucky bloke." Sadness weighs down his handsome features. My heart goes out to him. I know what it's like to feel that alone.

I know what it's like.

Suddenly, Verus's plan becomes clear. Epsilon is right. Verus did send me here. I'm supposed to convince Tempest to become my Gatherer.

I lift my gaze to meet Tempest's. "The man I care about is loyal and loving. He's my friend and partner." I run my fingertip by my eye. "We've both been Marked, too. Everyone thinks that we're doomed to become a certain type of demon. But we fight that together."

Tempest's eyes widen with disbelief and something else, too. "You're a team."

"Yes. And having someone on your side? It's the best feeling in the world."

Tempest hisses with pain and grips his right arm with his left. Without thinking, I set my hand on his shoulder. "Are you all right?"

Tempest nods. When he speaks again, his voice is thick with emotion. "Who are you?"

"I'm the one Verus told you about. I'm Portia."

His gaze turns intense. "But Verus said you hadn't been born yet."

"She's right. She sent me here to see you." I rest my free palm on Tempest's cheek. The touch makes us both tremble. "I didn't know why at first. Now, I do. I'm here to give you a message. There's more for you in life than what you have now. There's me. I love you so much, Tempest. Please come gather my heart. I'm waiting for you."

A genuine and intense look washes over his face. I can't stop smiling. "Now, there's my Tempest."

My trip through time abruptly ends. The party, the music, and Tempest all disappear. I've returned in the present day, standing in an empty ballroom. Footsteps sound behind me.

"I came to gather you, Portia. Just like you asked."

My eyes sting with happy tears. I turn around to see Tempest—my Tempest—standing on the other side of the empty ballroom in his battle gear. I race over to him and wrap my arms around his neck. "I love you."

"And I've loved you from the first time we met."

He steps away and rolls up the right sleeve of his Henley. There's a pattern to his armscales. I gasp as I recognize the tribal marks that arch around my eyes. "I'm mated, Portia. My dragon chose you the first time we spoke. In that moment, I decided to become your Gatherer. I've spent the years since working hard to be ready for the love that I saw in your eyes."

My breath catches. He worked and waited for twenty years. The loneliness must have been so hard. "Why didn't you find me before? We didn't have to talk about the Firmament."

"Verus. Like I said, she had very specific instructions. I couldn't see you without putting everything at risk. That was a risk I couldn't take. Dragons mate for life."

I inhale a shocked breath. "You mean, you waited for me for twenty years?"

"What else could I do? You're my mate. My Rhana." He steps closer and sets his palm on my cheek, like I did to him at the ball. "I want to share my life with you, if you'll have me." His gaze turns intense. "I want you to be my Empress."

My mind stalls out. Of all the things that Tempest would say tonight, asking me to be his Empress didn't even make the list. "I don't know what to say."

"Take your time, Portia. I know this is a lot to take in." He gently runs his finger along my jawline. "You'll have plenty of time to think about it."

A low tremor moves across the floor. Windows rattle in their frames. Chandeliers sway and clatter. Another sinkhole is forming. Tempest's last words echo through my mind.

You'll have plenty of time to think about it.

My insides twist with worry. Time is what we're running out of. "I'm afraid we have to hold off on that conversation for now. We need to find that last seedpod, Tempest."

"I know." He lowers his hand. "Let's get you suited up."

A knock sounds at the ballroom door. Tempest and I share a surprised look.

"Is anyone else here?" I ask.

"No," says Tempest. "I sent all the guards outside."

The door swings open. Alden steps inside. "Hey, guys."

Shock and anger cloud my brain. "How did you get in here?"

Alden offers me an easy smile. "I told you I had some magic saved up for a rainy day."

"That's more than a little magic," says Tempest with a frown. "I've warded this place to the hilt."

I set my hand on Tempest's shoulder. "However you got in here, you weren't invited. I thought I make it clear that you needed to stay away."

Scales appear over Tempest's skin as he pulls me against his side. "You heard Portia. Go."

"I will go, I swear. I just came to warn you."

"We don't need it," says Tempest.

I set my palm against Tempest's chest. The drum of his heart is beating at double time. "Alden's helped us before." I remember how he saved those quasis and brought news about my family. "Go on."

"It's about the Scintillion," says Alden quickly. "He's smarter than he looks. If he hasn't killed you by now, he'll go after someone you care about."

I can't help but chuckle. "Then good luck to him. My family would like nothing better than to go after a Class A demon."

Tempest pulls me against him more tightly. "Why are you telling us this?"

"Because, believe it or not, I do care if your quest succeeds. Just be ready, that's all. The Scintillion counts on the element of surprise for his plan to work." He rubs his neck and looks awkwardly around the empty ballroom. "That's it. Good luck to you both. Not that you need it. You two are doing a great job."

I'm starting to feel awkward, too. Alden's making a real effort here. *Maybe I've misinterpreted him all along?* "Thank you, Alden."

"Any time." Alden starts to walk away, pauses, and turns around to face us again. "One last thing. I want to apologize for acting like a psychopath before. Being one of the Marked isn't exactly a low-stress job and I lost it. Sorry."

"I understand, Alden." And I do. I've been living in a pressure cooker of the Void and the Firmament all my life.

"Thanks." He whispers a quick incantation and disappears.

I scrub my face with my hands. Just when I think things can't get any stranger, I'm sent back in time, tell Tempest I love him, get proposed to in return, and then have a close encounter with someone who's either a psychopath or just really stressed out. If we live through this quest, I'm taking a year-long vacation, minimum.

But in the meantime, I have to change into my

battle gear and head for the Grove. The final seedpod awaits.

Chapter Eighteen

Once again, Tempest and I stand in the Grove before the four Sacred Trees. Every few seconds, the ground trembles. Bits of earth tumble from the ceiling. My heart rate goes at double speed.

We need to finish the job and fast.

I pull the wicker sphere from around my neck and set it onto my palms. "We're in the Grove now," I say to the orb. "Where's the last seedpod?"

The strands of the sphere twist into the massive proportions unique to a Sacred Tree. I run my fingers over the intricate model. "Looks like the seedpod is under one of the trees."

Tempest nods. "I'll check them."

"Thanks. I'd help but I tend to get stuck."

"No worries." Tempest tests out the ground beneath each of the trees. At the fourth one, the lines of his shoulders tense. "I think I found it." He digs into the soil, clearing away the earth. The top of an oval of rock appears. "And there you are."

I kneel beside him to get a closer look. What I see makes me suck in an uneasy breath. "This one's bigger than the others." That makes sense, considering that Purgatory is the focal point between the other realms. It needs more energy to do its job.

Memories flicker through my mind. Everything went smoothly when we opened the seedpod in Furonium. Even so, with this much energy at play? Anything could happen. "Maybe we should try something different this time."

"Name it, luv." Another tremor rocks the ground. "Only best be quick."

"I'm worried about the extra energy in this thing. Last time, we were able to control the seedpod because we worked our magic together."

"Yes, Furor and Firmament."

"What if we try a different spell this time? One that specifically combines our powers."

"The idea has merit." Tempest rubs his jawline, his gaze lost in thought. "Let's try a fusing spell. There's a Furor one that starts off 'arrah kaz.' We can raise our arms with the second verse. That will give an extra boost of power."

"I know that spell. It's perfect."

The ground rolls more violently than ever before. The movement reminds me of a blanket being snapped over a bed. A huge chunk of rock tumbles from the ceiling, landing only a few feet away. My pulse kicks into high gear. "Let's do this." I hop to my feet.

Standing side by side, Tempest and I begin the incantation. Our voices mix, his tones deep and rolling, mine gentle and high. The air becomes charged with our unique magic. I raise my right arm parallel to the ground. Tempest does the same and sets his hand atop mine. Our combined voices grow louder as we summon the seedpod out of the earth.

The earth surrounding the fourth tree begins to shimmy. Tension rolls up my spine. *Please, let this work.* With a great heave, a circular rock breaks through the ground and settles before the tree. We raise our voices; the casting grows even more powerful. The orb's stone shell shatters, revealing the largest sphere of golden light yet. Tempest and I start the final verse of the incantation, which is supposed to close down the spell. That isn't what happens.

Instead, our joined powers feed off each other. Tempest's Furor strength pulls more liquid magic from my soul. Droplets of golden power appear on our fingertips. As we finish off the spell, the fluid energy cascades from our hands onto the golden orb. It pulses more brightly.

Our spell finishes at last. The liquid energy disappears from our hands. Tempest and I share a long glance, and there's a whole conversation hidden in that gaze.

"Did we dream that?" I ask.

"No, that really happened. We sent energy into the seedpod."

I raise my hand and stare at my palm. Amazing. In all my research, I've never come across anything like this.

The ground flutters again as the rest of the golden orbs break through the earth. Like the sphere for Purgatory, they all come to rest at the bases of their trees. Tempest and I stop speaking or even moving.

All our attention becomes riveted on the four yellow orbs. The spheres have turned impossibly bright. Everything around us—from the trees and twigs to the roots and soil—looks pale and almost yellow-white in the intensity.

Anticipation hangs thick in the air. Something is happening. Is this when the Firmament will finally get healed?

Each glowing sphere shifts and lengthens. My limbs quiver with excitement. The orbs continue their transformation until they take on a humanoid shape. My eyes widen with shock.

Those yellow orbs are actually living beings.

Each golden figure is curled into a fetal position at the base of a tree. Their backs turn toward the ceiling, while their arms and legs are tucked neatly beneath them. I shake my head in amazement. Tempest reaches out and grips my hand tightly. He's just as overwhelmed as I am.

The figures start to move.

Acting in unison, the four beings stand. There are two men and two women. Every inch of their bodies glows with golden light. The men are tall, slim, and broad-shouldered. They have shaved heads and youthful faces with wide, alien-looking eyes. The men have linen kilts wrapped around their waists and thin sandals on their feet. The women are lithe and willowy with long plaited hair and dainty features. Their Egyptian-style sheaths are covered in tiny crystals. The beads on the dress of the last woman—the figure for Purgatory—shine with so much power, I have to shield my vision when I look at them.

Everything in the Grove takes on a dreamlike

sheen. I blink quickly, not believing what I'm seeing. When I cast the Firmament spell at my penthouse, the incantation worked best with canopic jars. I never would've guessed *this* was the reason.

The four figures start to move.

Acting in sync, they turn around, stopping once they face the trees behind them. Raising their right arms, they touch the tree bark with the tips of their pointer fingers. A bright dot of light appears where their fingertips connect with the bark. The four lower their hands and draw luminescent lines down the length of the trees.

My mouth falls open with surprise and wonder. Tempest pulls me closer against him. When he speaks, his voice is hushed and reverent. "Stunning."

I try to find words to describe the wonder I feel, but there are none. I can only nod in agreement.

The lines of light suddenly blaze brighter. After that, the trees split open, revealing their dark and hollowed-out centers. The four beings slowly turn to face us once more.

"We are the Radiant," they say in unison. Their voices hold everything from the tinkling of bells to the rumbling of the earth. The sound is beautiful, ethereal, and unforgettable. "We rejuvenate the Sacred Trees."

My Princess training kicks into action. "Pleased to meet you."

In a bird-like movement, they all tilt their heads and focus on me. "You are the Marked. You must finish our work. Cast a growing spell."

My shoulders slump with relief. A growing spell? Now that, I can handle. I could do those back when saying two-word incantations took me days. Now that I can tap into the power of the Firmament, I should be able to manage it, no problem.

"Yes, I can cast a growing spell."

"And I'll help," says Tempest. Based on the steel in his voice, the topic is not up for discussion.

The Radiant nod in reply. After that, they all step backward, moving to stand directly inside the opened trees behind them. Their bodies cast a warm glow within the hollow trunks. The Radiant all fold their arms across their chests. The position reminds me of mummies in a sarcophagus.

A dark realization comes into focus. This is how humans used canopic jars in ancient Egypt. Something that once contained life had to go inside the jars in order to make them work. Now, the Radiant will be sealed inside the trees, their life force slowly drained to sustain the Firmament.

The Radiant fix their luminescent eyes on me. The heavy bark closes around their feet. The trees continue to seal around them, higher and higher. The trees soon fasten around their ankles and knees.

I wince in sympathy. No one knows canopic jar magic like I do. The trees will slowly pull energy from the Radiant. That kind of transfer hurts like hell.

The bark closes over their waists. The faces of the Radiant twitch with held-in pain. Their hands tremble in their crossover position. The bark then closes over their faces. All their mouths become frozen in silent screams.

For a full minute, I can only stare at the four Firmament trees. Worry prickles across my skin. The Radiant are all inside, but the trees remain bare and spindly. Their thin branches look like skeletal arms that reach up for help. My stomach sinks. The Firmament is not healed. I need to do what the Radiant asked.

"We have to cast that growing spell now," I say.

"Which one?" asks Tempest.

"Let's try another Furor incantation. There's one that begins with 'rah krall.'"

"I know it."

Together, we begin the spell. This time, Tempest's power is strong, but my Firmament energy is strangely weak. Something is off. I can barely tap into a faint trickle of power. An unsettled feeling weighs down my bones. We finish the incantation and wait. The quiet of the Grove rings loudly in my ears.

Will this work? Have we finally done it?

The ground trembles. A low rumble echoes through the forest. My heart skips a beat or two. Is that the sign of a sinkhole… Or of something far better?

The scent of fresh earth fills the air. The four Firmament trees start to grow. Their branches thicken with health. Roots twist deep into the soil, making the ground shimmy. Their trunks rise a few feet into the air.

And then, they all stop. Everything turns silent. Long moments tick by. Nothing else happens. Threads of doubt wind through my thoughts.

"Do you think we did it?" I ask.

"I'm not sure," says Tempest.

I stare at the trees, willing them to move. They don't budge. The ground shifts, though. Small sinkholes punch through the Grove floor. Adrenaline and alarm charge through me. The Firmament trees lurch at odd angles.

My skin chills over with shock. The trees are turning black and dying. I can't let that happen. My mind races through the quest. There must be some clue. This can't be the end.

"What did we miss?" I ask Tempest. My voice cracks with desperation.

"I don't know, luv."

That's when I see it. A thin sapling stands in the center of the ring of Sacred Trees. It wasn't there a few minutes ago.

A growing spell. My eyes widen as I realize what the Radiant really meant. The Firmament needs a new tree.

The truth hits me with a wallop. My spell back home used canopic jars and a pentagram. The five-pointed star was the key to the spell. A fifth source of energy is the key to reviving the Firmament. And I've always held Firmament power inside me. It's been so anxious to come out, it tied my tongue up every time I tried to use a different kind of power.

A weight of despair presses in around me. To heal the after-realms, I must power the final tree. My eyes sting with held-in tears. I can't stop picturing all the things I'll miss. Tempest and I getting married. Holding our newborn baby. Watching our grandchildren grow up.

My mind goes into shock. My body feels frozen and numb. I stumble over to the fifth tree.

Tempest's gaze flips between the sapling and me. Understanding tightens his features. He steps up to me, spins me to face him, and grips my shoulders tightly. "There must be another way, Portia. We can cast another spell."

"That will only help the tree grow; it won't be enough to keep it alive and save the after-realms. I have to go inside that thing." I set my hand against his cheek. His skin trembles with misery. "This is for everyone I love, including you."

Tempest nods. The look of grief in his gaze is so intense, my heart almost breaks.

"Let's start another incantation," I say softly.

His eyes glisten with tears. "What spell, Rhana?"

"The Furor have one for trees."

Tempest nods, his mouth a thin line of mourning.

I slide my hand in his and together we begin the spell. Our chanting fills the air. The ground beneath us stops shifting. No more sinkholes form. The thin green sapling springs higher out of the soil, quickly growing into a mighty tree whose branches disappear into the loosely packed ceiling of earth.

For a long second, I can only stare at the rich brown bark before me. This tree is full of life. But even now, I can sense its power draining. It needs more life within it to grow. A shudder rolls up my neck. How long will I trapped inside?

The Grove quakes with more force than ever before. Great boulders slam into the ground nearby. Time has run out. It doesn't matter what price must be paid.

I will do this. Now.

It takes all my strength to stand before the new tree. Raising my hand, I set my pointer finger against the bark. Firmament energy moves through me once again, igniting my fingertip with golden power. I lower my arm, opening up the tree as the Radiant did. The dark center gapes before me.

I steel my shoulders, turn around, and step backward into the tree trunk. Like the other Radiant, I fold my arms across my chest. My nerves are so on edge, it's hard to breathe.

The tree encircles my feet and calves, crushing my bones. I let out a cry of pain.

Tempest quickly rises to stand. Leaning forward, he braces his arms on either side of the tree. His gaze is steady and strong as it locks with mine. "I know this hurts, Rhana. Keep looking at me."

I try to hold our gaze; it's a struggle. More magical energy gets pulled from my skin. It's as if hundreds of needles have plunged into me at once, drawing power away from my veins and moving it into the Firmament. My legs become fully encased in the tree. Pain shoots up my spine.

Tempest keeps my gaze, his eyes lined with tears. "Know this, Rhana. I'll find a way to free you. I'll never give up."

Bark crawls across my chest. The agony slices into my ribs like knives. I close my eyes against the pain.

"Right here, luv. Look at me."

"It's hard, Tempest. It hurts."

"Then, it hurts me, too."

Another kind of pain gets added into the mix. Looking into Tempest's eyes, I see all that we're losing. Birthday parties. Late night kisses. Breakfast in bed. "We'll miss… So much."

"Not everything." His mouth trembles as he forces a smile. "My offer, remember?"

I know what offer he's talking about. He asked me

to become his Empress. I may be entering an eternity of pain, but yes, I'll take him up on this. I'll give myself this one consolation.

"Yes, Tempest." My voice quivers with pain. "I'll be your Empress."

Tempest kisses me once, gently. "One way or another, we'll be together. This isn't the end."

But everything is over, and we both know it. The bark crawls up my throat, pressing in on my windpipe. My mouth falls open in a silent scream as it encases my mouth, nose and eyes. Firmament magic burns every cell in my body though with agony.

I am locked in.

My world transforms into a nightmare of darkness and pain. I stay alive but not breathing. Immobile but not dead. There's only one consolation in this agony.

I am his Empress.

A fresh wave of magical energy moves through me. This power is different. It reminds me of Tempest, but it springs from deep within me. The energy is strong and structured. It fights against the power of the Firmament.

This is Furor energy, and it surrounds my soul like a mountain of power. As the Furor magic in me grows, my Firmament energy goes berserk. The tree lurches painfully around me. My mind goes to the man who promised to always stay at my side.

Tempest. Help me, Tempest.

My new Furor power strengthens my rage. I writhe inside my tomb. The bones in my arms break. My ribs and jaw crack. The ear-splitting sounds shatter the quiet of my tomb. Agony spikes through me, body and soul.

I don't belong here. *I need out!*

With a loud crack, the wood around my wrists shatters. Warm hands grip mine. It's Tempest. He speed-casts spells as he smashes through the wood with his bare hands and tail, dragging me out of the tree and cradling me into his lap. My fighting suit is a ruin of torn rags.

"Portia, luv. Say something."

"I failed. I tore up the Sacred Tree. The after-realms…"

Around us, all the trees wobble with the force of another sinkhole. Tempest carefully brushes the bits of dirt and debris from my face. "What happened?"

"I just kept thinking that I'm your Empress and…"

More dragon-like energy pummels through me. This time, the power is so strong, it sends a new and burning pain through every nerve I've got. The skin on my hands feels like it's on fire. I hold up my fingers. My heart fills with grief and dread.

I've escaped one kind of eternal death only to fall into another one.

My hands are turning black, just like I saw in the dream catcher. I'm turning into a Void demon.

"It's happening," I choke out.

Tempest cups my hand within his own, his face blank with surprise. "No. This can't be."

Hot tears well in my eyes. *Everything I've done has collapsed into failure.* The after-realms are doomed. And now, I'll spend my last minutes turning into the very demon I've dreaded my entire life. My hand completely blackens, as well as my arm.

"Leave me, Tempest. I won't let the last thing I do be hurting you."

He shakes his head, his face still unreadable. "You won't hurt me."

Another shot of hot pain drives through my stomach. I curl forward in agony. "You don't know that. I'm turning into a Void demon. I'll do anything."

"You're turning into a demon, Portia, but not the Void."

"What?"

"Look." He reverently runs his fingers over my skin. "This isn't the black ooze of a Void demon. You're getting armscales."

Armscales. The word sticks in my mind. All the full-blooded Furor have armscales. I run my fingers over my changing skin. Surprise twists through my stomach.

Tempest is right. "How is this possible?"

"Remember seeing me in the dream catcher as a lad? I was a scrawny thing. When I accepted my role as Emperor I changed."

More pain slices into me; I push past it. Tempest gained powers when he became a greater demon. Could that be happening to me as well? Both the energy of the Firmament and the Furor run through my soul. The new combination of magic goes to work. My bones knit back together. Strength returns to my limbs.

Dragon scales now cover me from head to toe. All my pain fades away. I run my hands up my arms, loving the leathery touch of the scales. My head and body feel woozy with power.

I'm one of the Furor.

A final transformation washes over my body. My scales slowly change from black to red. I look at Tempest, confused.

"Is this right?" I ask.

"Yes, luv. Only the Empress has red scales."

The power inside me stops expanding and changing. My body and mind become calm. "Is it over?"

"Yes."

I brush by the corner of my eye. "And the marks?"

"Still there. Still beautiful."

I inspect my body, wondering if anything else has changed. I appear to be the same size and shape as before. My armscales match Tempest's, only his are black with red, and mine are red with black. Something taps my shoulder. I look over to see the arrowhead end of a tail. My tail.

"I'm Furor," I say, my voice low with awe.

"More than that. You're a greater demon. What power did you gain in the transformation? Can you sense any difference?"

I close my eyes and search my soul. Every part of me is bursting with life and magic. I never imagined this much power was possible.

"Yes, it's like that spell we cast on the last seedpod. When we combined our two energies, we ended up with more." I shake my head, searching for some way to describe this. "It's like one and one make three. Does that make sense?"

"Perfectly."

The ground around us rumbles more violently than ever before. Huge chunks of the ceiling cave in. A crack splits the first Firmament tree. Despair crushes in around me. I'm now with the man I love as his Empress, and I'll only have enough time to die at his side.

My new powers churn through me. At first, I sense the framework of Furor magic within my soul. Soon, the power multiplies. Furor magic solidifies through me. More strength and energy builds. A realization forms. My heart skips a beat. Maybe two. "I may know a way out of this!"

"What, luv?" A sinkhole crumbles the ground beneath his feet. He barely jumps away in time. "I'm up for anything."

"Before, you asked if we could cast a spell to power my Sacred Tree. I said we didn't have enough energy to get the job done. But now?" I feel giddy with excitement. "We might be able to do it. We can use the same spell and everything."

Tempest grabs my hand and drags me toward the ruin of my Sacred Tree. I set my palm into the center of the hollowed-out trunk. Tempest places his hand against mine. We cast the spell together, louder and faster this time. We summon the same liquid energy that dripped from our fingertips when we opened the last seedpod.

Rivulets of golden power curl down our arms. The liquid energy falls off our outstretched palms, filling the base of the tree. It greedily soaks in the magic and begins to heal itself. Long branches reach up into the packed earth above our heads. Golden power fills the tree's empty core. The torn bark sutures itself together. The trunk elongates and glows with power.

Tempest and I lower our arms and step away from the tree. Our spell is over. The Grove quiets. The earthquakes stop.

The other trees burst with light and growth. Their roots and branches turn blazingly bright. The surrounding forest becomes green and lively. The grove transforms from a dank underground chamber into a place of light and life.

A sense of peace permeates the air. The trees glow more brightly than ever before. The energy inside them thrives. I wrap my arms around Tempest's neck and pull him into a tight hug. "We did it, Tempest!"

He nuzzles my ear. "That was a brilliant idea."

Joy balloons through my chest. "As a wise man said, we make a great team."

"He's just wise, then?"

I bob my head, thinking. "Oh, he might have a cute butt, too."

"He does?" His gives me one of his crooked smiles. My knees go wobbly.

"Among other things."

Tempest runs his finger down my cheek. "How are you feeling, luv?"

"Good. Better than good. Great."

"And your Firmament magic?"

I close my eyes, reaching out to the magic in my soul. I sense the strong power of the Furor magic along with the liquid energy of the Firmament. Excitement tingles through my stomach. "I still have it. I can cast with both now."

I shake my head. After so many years of struggling to cast, now I can access two kinds of magic. I wind my arms around Tempest's waist, pulling us into a tighter hug. There's a thrill of connection as his arms wrap around me.

"My Rhana," says Tempest.

A wave of warmth rolls up my spine. Looking over, I see that my tail has entwined itself with Tempest's. The sight makes me smile with anticipation. This is the first of many things we'll learn about each other. My heart soars.

"You're my Rhana, too."

Chapter Nineteen

A guttural snarl breaks though the quiet of the Grove. Shock careens though my limbs. I pull away from Tempest.

"It's the Scintillion," I say. "He's here."

Tempest's skin becomes covered with dragon scales. "He won't be for long."

Alden stumbles into the clearing. His clothes are torn and bloody. Half his face is swollen with bruises. "Portia… I came to warn you… the Scintillion." His eyes roll into his head as he collapses onto the ground.

I rush to kneel his side. "Alden, are you all right?"

His lids pop open. His features turn bright with triumph. "Now, I am." He grabs my wrist. I try to twist free, but he's already casting his transport spell. The world around me disappears.

# # #

When everything comes back into focus, I find

myself lying on my back in a graveyard. Damn. This is the same spot as last time. Alden stands a few yards away, puffing on a cigarette. His face and clothes are still a mess.

I roll myself into a seated position. My new tail starts to stir under my long leather duster. On reflex, I set my hand atop the arrowhead end. My tail quiets. Until I know what's going on, I don't want to announce how I've changed.

I look into Alden's smug face. *What a chump I've been.* "I can't believe I fell for that trick again."

"Oh, I can." Alden takes another pull from his smoke. "I figured that after a little bleeding heart action, you'd be dumb enough to get close."

My brows lift with surprise. Who is this guy and what happened to Alden? The helpful man who's been begging for a second chance is gone. Now, Alden glares at me with a predatory air, like he's a lion and I'm raw meat. A chill creeps up my neck.

Danger.

I scan the clouds. *Should I attack, run, or wait for Tempest?*

"You can watch the skies all you want," says Alden. "Your boyfriend won't show." He takes one last drag off his cig before stubbing it out on a tombstone. "I cast a ton of wards over this place. It'll take him a year to break through."

I worry my lower lip with my teeth. If backup isn't coming, then I need to deal with this myself. Closing my eyes, I search for magic in my soul. I brace myself for the onslaught of combined Furor power and Firmament energy.

Nothing comes.

I frown, confused. Maybe I need a different tactic. I try an old-fashioned word-based spell instead. I can't get that out, either. Alarm charges through my nerves. "You blocked my magic."

Alden casually brushes some dirt off his loafers. "I had to protect myself. Level One spells are pretty lame. Still, you might cause me trouble."

My shoulders slump with relief. Alden doesn't know that I can do advanced magic. That's a good thing. The fact that I'm now Furor is a secret. I file that fact away.

For now, I need a way to fight. I pat the holster on my thigh. It's empty. I curse under my breath. Alden took my dagger, too. My pulse thuds faster. *I'm completely defenseless before this creep.*

Calm down Portia. What did they teach you on demon patrol?

We covered situations like this in training. My best bet is to try and get him talking. That way, I can stall for time and come up with a plan. "Why am I here?"

Alden shrugs. "That's easy. We never got a chance to have our little ceremony. Will you go willingly this time? Or do I have to persuade you?" He cups his hand by his mouth. "I'll give you a hint. The persuading part will hurt."

His cold stare ties my stomach into knots. *Think, Portia.*

My mind whips through options at top speed. Tempest always talks about his inner dragon. Now I have one, too. The timing couldn't be better. Closing my eyes, I search for the dragon inside me. There's nothing. I try again. Same thing. Disappointment weighs down my shoulders. Maybe it's too early for me to use my powers.

Alden chuckles darkly. "Starting to realize your options are about zero, huh?"

A chill curls up my spine. *He's right.*

Alden snaps his fingers in a 'come here' motion. "We're leaving, Portia. Now."

I take a cautious step backward. "I'm not going anywhere with you."

"You are, and I'll tell you why." He rubs his hands together. "I captured the Scintillion."

My breath catches. The Scintillion? I just healed the Firmament. With the Scintillion at large, it won't take long before it's torn apart again. I scan Alden's gloating face. *This could all be another trap.* "How can I believe you? You've kidnapped me twice now. And you just threatened me, too."

"Guess you'll have to come with me and see for yourself." He tilts his head. "Or are you willing to put the Firmament at risk again?"

I huff out a worried breath. If Alden has some news on the Scintillion, then I need to find out what it is. "Okay. I'll go."

Alden kicks off his tombstone. "Now, was that so hard?" He hikes off into the mist. "Follow me!"

I trail him through a series of neat graveyards covered in thick mist and grass. As I trudge along, my researcher's brain goes to work. *I'm missing something, I know it.* A fact rises to top of mind. Alden once said that he only has a little residual Firmament magic left. But today, he cast wards strong enough to block both Tempest and my powers. Alden could never do that with leftovers. He's been getting a regular infusion of Firmament magic, and on a huge scale, too. More pieces of the story fall into place. Alarm slams into me as I realize the truth.

Like a sleepwalker, I stumble along behind Alden. My head feels fuzzy. We end our hike in a valley that's filled with open graves. Alden waits for me at the first tombstone. "And here we are."

The words tumble out of my mouth on their own. "You're the Scintillion, aren't you?"

Alden grins. Little by little, he slides his open palm down his face. The motion acts like a magical zipper opening. One second, Alden's a regular guy. The next, he's the Scintillion. My blood chills.

Alden swipes his huge claw upward, and he looks human again. Only this time, he doesn't have a scratch on him. He does a golfer's clap at me. "And the Princess solves our first mystery. But will she figure out the rest?"

My mind whirls through different scenarios. I picture Alden being chosen as one of the Marked. He can play the nice guy really well, but that's only skin deep. My hands curl into fists. "You never even opened a seedpod, did you? You figured out how to steal the Firmament magic instead."

Alden quirks his brow. "Good job, Portia. You're not as dumb as you look."

The rest of the pieces tumble in place. "When you wouldn't take on the quest, you turned into a Void demon. Every time a new Marked came to the Grove, you attacked them and siphoned off their power, didn't you?"

Alden gestures to an opened grave. "See for yourself."

Warning bells go off in my head. *Watch out for another trick, Portia.* With hesitant steps, I walk to the nearest tombstone. It's a thin white slab of stone with two words scratched on it: "Marked #23."

My body chills over with alarm. *Is Alden burying the Marked here?*

A rasping groan sounds from inside the open grave. Every instinct I have tells me to run. But I can't. If something happened to the other Marked, then I need to know that, too. I force my gaze down.

A Void demon lies twitching on the bottom of the grave. Its features are contorted in pain. My heart cracks. This poor soul failed its quest and turned into a Void demon. What a tragedy. All this person wanted to do was help the after-realms. Now, they're trapped in a nightmare.

I scan the graveyard. All the blood drains from my face. "You did this to hundreds of people."

"Right again," says Alden. "The Firmament was low on energy—I blew off my quest, after all—so the Grove kept sending in new Marked to start their own quests." He makes little quotations marks with his fingers when he says quests. "Chumps, all of them. I took their power and liked what I got."

My jaw clenches. "I can't believe this. The after-realms were falling apart because of you!"

Alden rolls his eyes. "There was never any real risk, Portia. I'd have given the Sacred Trees enough juice when the time came. I can take as well as give. It's just that I don't always feel like it."

His words make my skin crawl. "Spoken like a true addict."

"This isn't addiction. This is a new power rising in

the after-realms."

"Sure, it is." I gesture across the lines of opened graves. "And I suppose you'll tell me that all this is a 'ceremony,' too." I make little quotation marks with my fingers when I say ceremony. *Take that.*

Alden's voice lowers to a growl. "It is a ceremony."

"No, it's a serial-killer style ritual for murdering innocent people." My voice drips with loathing. "You make me sick."

Alden defiantly raises his chin. "I take care of the Void. I give them everlasting life."

I remember the Void demon twitching in its grave. "No, you don't give them life. You control them like zombies."

Alden's mouth becomes a slash of anger. "I've been patient. That patience is running out."

My brows furrow with thought. Alden hasn't attacked me yet. That can only mean one thing. "You want something from me. You brought me here to scare me. That way, I'll tell you whatever you want to know. What is it?"

"Fine." He curls his hand and huffs out a breath on his nails. "I'm tired of being at the mercy of someone else for more power." He wags his finger at me. "You've been a naughty one, Portia. You've done something to Firmament magic. You healed that Sacred Tree without getting trapped in its trunk. I want to know what you did. And I want that power, too."

A knot of alarm tightens in my chest. Alden wants to know the secret of combining Firmament and Furor magic. He'd never be the equal of Tempest and me, but the creep is right. He could get a transfusion of Furor magic and cause some serious damage. I can't let that happen.

I keep my face carefully neutral. "Who says I did anything?"

"Don't play games. I'm going to drain your power and kill you, make no mistake. But if you tell me what I want to know, I'll let you die clean." He scans me from head to toe, a sick smile on his lips. "Maybe I'll even keep you alive for a while. We could have some fun together before it's over." He licks his lips. "You're a beautiful woman, Portia."

Nausea and fury move through me in waves. "Never."

Alden loosens the top two buttons on his shirt while bobbing his brows up and down. "Last chance."

My hands clench into fists. This creep is the biggest threat the after-realms have ever faced. "How about we try another deal? I kill you instead."

Wow. Did that come out of my mouth? Why yes, yes it did. And it felt really good, too.

"And here I thought you might be smart." He transforms into his demon form, leans back, and lets out an earth-shaking roar.

Every inch of my body tingles with adrenaline. I've got one option when it comes to fighting. I need to change into a dragon, fast. Trouble is, I have no idea how to do it.

Alden lumbers toward me. My breath quickens. I close my eyes and call to the Furor energy inside. Nothing happens.

Alden swipes his opened hand toward my head. I dodge at the last second and run. While I search for a good hiding spot, I whisper incantations for transformation. Just like before, the words can't get past my lips. Panic speeds down my spine.

Pounding footsteps sound behind me in the mist. The Scintillion is closing in. There are no large tombstones here, and I can't hide in one of the opened graves. With my mind blurring from panic, I reach for my inner dragon one more time.

I sense her. At last.

My dragon stirs in my soul and wow, is she ever pissed. All I get from her is mindless rage. I try to coax her with soft words.

I need you. Please take form.

The Scintillion finds me instead. I sprint off in a new direction, but he pounds his fist hard into my back. I tumble face-first onto the grass. Pain and panic slam into me with equal force. I plead with my dragon.

Get out and fight!

Suddenly, her battle rage ricochets through my body. Strength pumps through my every cell. My bones snap. Scales appear. Fangs grow. I gain a long neck, huge body, and spiked tail. I look down on the Scintillion from a new height.

I've become a massive red dragon.

The Scintillion roars with rage and rushes toward me. I call out to my dragon once more.

Give me fire.

My dragon guides me again. Instantly, I know what to do. I suck in a deep breath while triggering flames in my chest. My lungs burn with held-in fire. As Alden closes in, I blast a shaft of bright red flame straight into his chest. He stops and shields his face.

Alden doesn't die, not that I expected him to. After all, he didn't get hurt when Tempest scorched him. But he does slow down enough for me to come up with another plan.

Please, let it work.

The last flames leave my lungs. Alden rushes me again. I do the same to him. My huge clawed feet tear up the uneven ground. Alden raises both arms. Razor sharp talons glint in the dim light.

As we get closer, I call on my new dragon instincts once more.

Help me fly.

Fresh instincts tell me exactly how to make my wings unfurl. They beat in a steady rhythm and lift me into the sky. I scoop Alden into my talons. I pump higher and higher, the Scintillion writhing in my clutch.

My plan is simple. Alden said that he cast wards and other spells around the graveyard. If I fly high enough, I'll break past the range of his spells. I'll be able to counter-attack with my own magic.

Up and up I climb. When I wing past a jagged line of mountains, I feel the magic flow back into my body once again. Joy pulses through my veins. I broke through Alden's barriers. My powers have returned, and I know just what to do with them.

Alden wanted to know how I healed the Sacred Tree. That gave me an idea. If I could use Furor and Firmament magic in order to change the tree, couldn't I change Alden, too? Instead of charging him with extra magic, I'll change him into a human.

I launch a similar spell to the one Tempest and I used to heal my Sacred Tree. Streams of energy flow inside me. The Furor power protects and structures the Firmament magic. Around me, the air shimmers with magic. Golden Firmament power drips down my claws and onto the Scintillion. Alden tries to consume the energy, but I block him with Furor magic.

Not happening, Alden. I focus the spell on transforming him, not energizing him. Alden writhes and roars in my grasp. He doesn't like that he isn't getting fed.

The spell takes its toll. Pumping my wings becomes a huge effort. Too much of my focus is going into transforming Alden. Every inch of me becomes tired and boneless. Gritting my teeth, I pump more of my magic into Alden. I chant one word over and over in dragon tongue.

Transform.

Alden flickers between demon and human shape. Adrenaline and excitement pour through me. With one last push of power, Alden changes back into a human. He's now smaller and more vulnerable. I'm having a hard time keeping him in my talons.

"What did you do to me?" he asks.

Satisfaction warms my chest. "I made it so you'll never hurt the Firmament again. You're human now, Alden. And you're staying that way. No more magic or powers." *On the plus side, you'll make lot of new friends in jail.*

"Don't be crazy. I'm the Scintillion." He wiggles in my grip. It's tricky to hold him without crushing him to death.

My limbs tremble with worry. Alden's really not getting that he's human now. "Be careful. I don't want to hurt you."

"You can't hurt me, you dumb bitch. No one can." Alden thrashes around so much, he slides from my grip and tumbles through the clouds.

"Alden, no!"

My pulse races. I dive after Alden, hoping to catch him midair. He's nowhere to be found. I wing my way around the mountain. Alden's body lies on a craggy ledge near the summit. Dead. It happened so quickly, the guy didn't even have time to scream.

Sadness weighs down my heart. This is the real reason demon patrol and I don't get along. Any loss of life feels like a tragedy to me.

I gently pick up Alden and take back to the air. His lifeless body hangs limp in my talons. What a waste. Alden had so many gifts and he only used them to take power into himself. What if he could have helped someone else for once?

The question sparks an idea in my mind. There might be a way that Alden's death can make things better for the Void demons. If I can turn Alden back to a human, maybe I can do the same for the Void, too. My eyebrows furrow as I think through the necessary spells.

My heart lightens. *It's possible.* There's just one catch. There are too many Void demons for me to do this alone. I need magical help.

Arcing in a new direction, I fly off in search of Tempest.

# # #

Tempest and I stand before the hundreds of open graves created by Alden. We're in human form now. I shiver in disgust and regret. "Let's try another scanning spell."

"We've cast it fifty times, luv. It's going to tell us the same thing."

Disappointment presses in around me. I know Tempest is right. These Void demons aren't like the Scintillion. Alden must have consumed so much power, it allowed him to transform back into human form. These Void aren't the same. The most Tempest and I can do is set their souls free.

I stiffen my spine. *No, there must be another option.* "Maybe we can bring in some other experts in magic. See if they have any ideas."

Tempest pulls me to his side. "Do you think there's a better expert out there on the Void than you?"

I lean into his touch and sigh. "If there were, I'd have found them years ago."

"And do you think anyone can deliver more magic to this spell than we can?"

Sadness tightens in my throat. "No, I don't."

A pained groan sounds from one of the opened graves. Tempest sighs. "These poor souls have suffered enough. Let's set them free, luv."

From the first time I faced the Void in the cornfield, I always felt that they weren't evil. Tempest is right. We have to do what we can to free them now. And since we can't give them their mortal lives back, we can at least start them on their after-lives. From there, their own past actions will determine their fate… Not the Scintillion. Alden is already meeting his afterlife. I doubt it will be pleasant.

Tempest softly kisses my temple. "Shall we use the

same spell we did on your Sacred Tree?"

"Yes." I slip my hand into his. His touch is warm and firm. Somehow, that gives me the strength to go on. I straighten my shoulders. Tempest and I begin the incantation. The combined energy comes back to us even more quickly this time. I sense the liquid magic building up behind us. It's as if the power knows what it's about to be used for and can't wait to start.

The energy turns so intense, the liquid force churns around my feet. Tempest and I share a small nod and raise our joined hands. A tidal wave of golden liquid energy rushes out from behind us and covers the ground with magic. One by one, ghosts rise from their graves and float off toward Purgatory. Their faces are calm, eyes closed in relief. The spell ends. A peaceful quiet overtakes the graveyard.

My shoulders slump. *We did it.* Suddenly, it's like I can't remember ever being so tired. My legs feel rubbery beneath me. I look to Tempest with half-open eyes. "Remember how I'm always saying there isn't time to rest?"

Tempest offers me a sleepy smile. That casting did a number on him, too. "Yes, luv?"

"Well, now I really need to rest."

"As my Empress commands."

And even though I'm so tired I could sleep standing up, there's no denying the jolt of joy those four words bring.

Chapter Twenty

Tempest and I knock on the door to Maxon's mead hall. After taking a quick nap, we headed off to my brother's cloud castle. The place is pretty stark. Gray brick walls, flagstone floors, and arched stone ceilings. Good news is that the doorman confirmed my family's here. At least, Alden didn't lie about that.

Footsteps sound on the other side of the door. "Who's there?"

"It's me, Portia."

The door whips open to reveal a very tired but very happy Mom. She wraps me in a huge hug. "Baby! You're safe!"

"We did it," I say breathlessly. "The Firmament's fixed."

Mom's thin arms keep an iron-tight grip on my shoulders. "I knew you could do it." She barely gives Tempest a glance. "Thanks for taking care of my baby." Mom calls over her shoulder. "Look, everyone! Our Portia is back!"

My family crowds into the doorway all at once. There's Pops and Grandma Cam. G and Dad. Hildy, Lianna, and Walker. I'm pulled into one hug after the next, and everyone asks the same question: "What happened?"

I finally pull away from their embraces. "We rejuvenated the Firmament. That's the short story, anyway. Everything should be fine now."

"That's my angel girl," says Pops. "I knew you could do it!"

"I wasn't alone." I grab Tempest's hand and pull him to my side. "Tempest helped me."

A voice pipes up from across the room. "Yeah, looks like he did."

For the first time, I notice Maxon standing in a far corner. He didn't come over to hug me hello or ask any questions about what happened with the Firmament. My brother folds his arms over his chest. He's wearing jeans, a T-shirt, and a look that could kill.

Tempest wraps his arm over my shoulder. "What do you mean by that, M?"

An electric sense of alarm charges through the air. No one seems to breathe anymore.

"Look, guys." I take a pointed step away from Tempest. "Maybe we should all be happy that the after-realms are safe now. No one's about to die in an apocalyptic fiasco. We even wiped out the Void, too. I think that's a great thing to focus on. Right, Maxon?"

My brother totally ignores me. Maxon keeps glaring hot death at Tempest. My pulse skitters out of control. Any kind of boyfriend interaction is new to me. But family and boyfriend turmoil is way out of my comfort zone. I scan the room for support. "What do you guys say? Don't you think we should be focusing on the world not ending?"

None of them meet my gaze. My eyes widen in shock. They aren't going to back me up on this one. When I speak, my voice is little more than a squeak. "What's the problem, guys?"

"I'll tell you what the problem is," says Maxon. "You're walking in the door holding hands with the greater demon of lust and wrath, who I happen to know is a messed up piece of work."

My jaw drops. "I can't believe this."

"No one's trying to take anything away from you," says Maxon. "You saved the after-realms. But I won't stand here and let it slide that you went ahead and did exactly what you promised you wouldn't do." He points at Tempest.

My neck muscles cord with held-in anger. "I'm an adult, Maxon. Things happened that changed my mind. How about asking a few questions before you go off on a tear?"

"Okay, I've got a question." Maxon rounds on Tempest. "Why'd you do it, T?"

Tempest's face is the picture of calm. "Do what, exactly?"

"How can you ask me that?" Maxon's body flies apart in a puff of smoke, only to re-form a second later, right in front of Tempest. "My sister has a goddamn tail, T!"

My tail, which had been swaying casually behind me, now stops cold. Embarrassment and rage battle it out inside me. I can't decide if I want to cast an invisibility spell or punch my brother in the nose.

Lianna takes a few careful steps toward Maxon. "Look, babe. We all need to stay calm here."

"I'm calm." Maxon cracks his neck from side to side. I know that move. It's what my brother does when he's about to kick someone's ass. And the way he's glaring at Tempest? There's not a lot of wiggle room about whose ass he's targeting.

"So, what do you have to say, T?" asks Maxon. "Why does my sister have a tail?"

"Hey." Once again, I step right between Maxon and Tempest. "I'm right here. Do you want to know why I have a tail? Ask me."

Maxon ruffles my hair like I'm twelve years old. "Don't worry. I was in line for the throne of Furonium. I know what a tail means." He glares at Tempest again. "Especially one with red scales."

The tension level spikes. Dad and Pops firm their bodies into battle stance. Mom's tail arcs menacingly over her shoulder. My brows lift in disbelief. Am I dreaming this? I just saved the after-realms and my family is freaking out about my choice in men? I glare at Maxon. "Can we not do this now, Maxon?"

"You don't get it," growls Maxon. "I still struggle with what Armageddon did to me in Hell. And that didn't even last a week. T had years with Chimera. Some things change you and there's no going back. He is not dragging you down with him." Maxon pokes Tempest in the chest. "What's really going on here? Couldn't handle it when I became an elemental? Then you should've talked to me. You don't go around screwing with my sister's head."

"That's enough!" Rage churns through me. I call on my inner dragon. She's there in a heartbeat. Red scales appear all over my skin. Crimson wings arch over my shoulders. My tail points directly at Maxon's nose. Finally, I have my brother's full attention.

"Don't think I don't know what's going on here." I gesture across the room. "With all of you. Mom and Gram, since when you do thank someone who saved my life with less enthusiasm than the guy who serves your coffee? And the rest of you, how come you're letting Maxon spout all this garbage?"

I pause, giving them a chance to speak. They don't. Their battle stances relax, but the wary looks stay on their faces. My blood heats.

"Well, if you won't answer, I will. You all told me not to judge on appearances, and now you're doing just that. Tempest is not a title. He's not whatever reputation he had twenty years ago." I stare right at Maxon. "And he's not whatever Chimera did to him. He's Tempest. He's a man who stood by me as a peer and partner throughout this whole ordeal. He's someone who has earned my heart and I can only be amazed that I've earned his as well."

I lean into Tempest's side. His arm winds around my waist. The touch is comforting. "We love each other. I'm his Empress. It's your choice whether to join in our happiness."

A long moment of silence follows. Emotions battle it out in my soul. Love for Tempest. Disappointment in everyone else. And a little sense of pride that no matter what happens, I said what I needed to.

Dad steps forward to break the silence. "I'm ashamed, Portia. I should have trusted you to make the right decision; you've a beautiful heart and a brilliant mind. For the record, you both have my blessing."

"You have my blessing, too," says G.

Pops comes next. "Your gram and I wish you all the best."

One by one, the rest of my family steps forward to add their good wishes. My heart warms. Once they're all done, it takes me a few seconds to pull myself together and reply. Even then, my voice breaks. I can only manage a few short words. "Thank you."

Maxon frowns. "I can't believe this." His body changes into smoke and wafts away. Fresh disappointment weighs down my heart. How can he do this?

Lianna turns to me. "Give Maxon some time. This brings up bad memories for him." She gives my hand a gentle squeeze. "Excuse me." Her body transforms into mist as she disappears after him.

I lean more deeply into Tempest's side. All the excitement's getting to me again. Tempest guides me toward the door. "Come away, Portia. You need your sleep."

I barely remember saying my goodbyes and stumbling out of Maxon's castle. I vaguely recall laying in Tempest's arms as he sprouted wings in his semi-human form and flew us back to Furonium. I can't recall being set into his bed, although I'm sure it happened. But there's one thing I'll never forget.

My new life started today and it has my family's blessing.

Chapter Twenty-One

Tempest and I stand on the roof of the Emperor's Palladium. It's a modern high-rise that's our center of operations. Below us, the red landscape of Furonium stretches out in every direction. A large crowd quietly waits by the base of the building. Anticipation charges the air. It's a big day.

Tempest and I wear special leathers for the occasion. Mine are red; his are black. Both sets are sleeveless to show the armscale pattern that marks us a mated pair.

As we stand side by side, Tempest rests his large hand on my lower back. Warmth radiates from his palm, sending shivers up my spine.

"Are you ready?" he asks, his voice growly and low. "It's a big moment and there's no cause to rush."

Tempest makes a good point. Am I ready to start the official Procession that will mark the beginning of my reign as Empress?

"You ready?" I ask.

"More than." Once again, Tempest's deep voice makes my toes curl. I've heard that voice while doing all sorts yummy things over the last two months. We're taking things slow and I couldn't be happier. I blush at the memories.

Tempest quirks his brows. "You with me, Portia?" The sly look in his eyes says he knows exactly where my mind was.

My blush deepens. "I'm ready, Tempest."

"Brilliant." Tempest winds his free arm up my neck, and pulls me in for a slow, hot, and mind-numbing kiss. My body heats with desire. Tempest leans back and meets my gaze. I shoot him a sly look of my own. "I thought we were talking about the Procession."

"Were we? I got a little muddled."

"Liar."

He points to his own face. "Lust demon."

Somewhere below us, a herald plays a regal tune on his silver trumpet. Electric excitement charges my nerves.

"That's my cue," I say.

Tempest kisses my cheek. "You'll ace this one, luv."

"Thanks." I step up to the building's edge. My heart pounds so hard, I think it could break out of my rib cage. A large crowd has gathered below. I cast a quick spell to enhance my voice, and then I'm ready to begin.

"I stand before you today, Empress Portia Phi Tau Xavionus Guritha Rixum." I pause and double-check that I got everything right. My name's become a sentence lately. "I am here with my Rhana, Emperor

Tau Epsilon Omicron Theta, to hereby declare that as of this date, I shall begin my official rule as Empress of Furonium."

No one does anything. The crowd below stays silent. I glance over at Tempest. "What did I miss?"

"The declaration."

I snap my fingers and point at his nose. "Right." I turn back to the crowd. "I hereby declare the following." I raise my arms high. "Let the Procession begin!"

The crowd leans back and tilts their heads up to the skies. Dragon scales crawl up all their necks and faces. Acting in unison, they let out a single roar. The air vibrates with the force of their cries.

Tempest and I take hold of each other's hands. Together, we race toward the edge of the roof. I focus on the warmth of his palm in mine, and not on the possibility of being a Portia-sized pancake if I can't manage this next bit properly.

Before I know it, Tempest and I have reached the building's edge. We leap forward. Air roars in my ears and whisks over my skin. I remind myself to try and picture my dragon form, but my body is already changing. It's like Tempest's been saying. My dragon nature has started to take over. Within seconds, I'm in my dragon form: red, long, and sturdy with a headdress of horns. I spread my wings and pump up toward the clouds.

The crowd goes berserk. Behind us, the Kathikon take to the skies as well.

Tempest flies along at my side. "Well done, Portia."

"I didn't do anything that time. It just happened

naturally."

"Which is why it was perfect."

There's an odd sensation as my extra-long mouth breaks into a smile across an impossible number of teeth. "Thank you."

"Now, we head east."

Tempest and I fly off for our first stop on our Procession through Furonium. This is Thornclaw territory. As our shadows pass above the fields, the Thornclaw lean back, roar their lungs out, and take to the skies. With the Thornclaw behind us, we move on to other lands. There are all-white dragons who hide in snowdrifts, Mindaray with wings as small as petals, and Electrophus who burst out from the red-tinted seas.

By the time Tempest and I start making our way back, there are so many dragons following us, our entourage darkens the skies. I feel like I could burst with exhilaration and pride. I'm leading my people in flight.

My people.

I've never thought that before about the thrax or the quasis, but now, that's the right word for the Furor.

Mine. Just like Tempest.

As we return to the Palladium, I can see the different balconies of the building are now filled with new people. My family is the final stop on my Procession. The Eastern balcony is crammed with thrax in their multi-colored gowns and tunics. My long dragon's throat constricts with joy. At the balcony's edge, there stands G, Walker, and Hildy. They wave at me, their faces beaming.

Tempest and I fly around to the Western balcony. This one's filled with quasis wearing purple. A multitude of tails wag or sway. My pulse jumps. Grandma Cam stands at the railing, waving to me. She wears her Presidential suit and purple sash of office.

Tempest and I swoop up over the top of the Palladium. There, we find my parents waiting for me, arm in arm. They're in full get-up as King and Queen. Dad's in a tunic with the Rixa eagle crest. Mom wears a black over-gown atop her white Scala robes. Silver crowns glisten atop their heads. When she sees me, Mom raises her arms high and summons a column of igni around her and Dad. The small lightning bolts of power swirl around my parents in a cyclone formation before climbing up into the clouds. Mom lowers her arms, and a gateway opens in the sky.

My dragon's mouth stretches into an even wider smile. Mom's opened a portal to Heaven.

The first to descend through the clouds is my grandfather Xavier. He's in full archangel mode with his golden wings, gleaming armor, and sword of white flame. Behind him follows a host of angels, their voices raised in song.

I discover something. You know who gets weepy around singing angels? Everyone. My eyes tear up instantly. I glance over to Tempest. "It's nice."

Don't cry, Portia. Keep it together.

Tempest lowers his voice. "By the by, this song is what they sang when Xav took office as archangel."

It was? And now, the blubbering starts. "That's…so…beautiful."

"Are you all right, luv?"

"Yes." I sniffle loudly. "I'm just so happy." I scan the scene, seeing everyone I love. Well, almost everyone. There are two very noticeable absences. My heart sinks. "Are Maxon and Lianna coming?"

"I'm so sorry, Portia."

I nod slowly. I haven't heard a word from Maxon since that day at his castle. Lianna keeps saying that he needs more time, and I understand that. But seeing this huge display from my whole family? It only makes me miss Maxon more. A guilty weight settles into my stomach. I should be thankful that my family's here. Plus, I'm alive, have Tempest, and have found a new home where I truly belong. The fact that my bullheaded brother isn't here shouldn't bother me.

Only, it does bother me. A lot.

My grandfather hovers beneath the singing choir, his golden wings beating out in time with the music. Pops' bright blue eyes catch my dragon stare, and I know he can guess my thoughts. He offers me a sad smile.

Hold it together, Portia.

Tempest nudges my neck with his dragon snout. "How about we call an end to the Procession? We need to get ready before the feast."

"That's a good idea."

And then, I see it.

Hazy shapes begin to appear on either side of Pops. My breath catches.

This can't be right. I must be seeing things.

The two forms come into clearer focus. On the left side of Pops, there now stands Lianna. She's in water elemental mode, so her body looks like it's made from swirling rain. I exhale with relief as I see who stands to Pops' right.

It's Maxon. He's here.

My brother is in full air elemental mode. His body appears to be made from curling smoke. He steps across the sky like anyone else would walk across the pavement. He pauses before me.

"Hey," he says.

Hey. How my brother can stuff a world of meaning into one word, I'll never know, but he always does.

"Hi."

"Look, I'm so sorry. I got mixed up in my own damn mess and I acted like a dick. Forgive me, yeah?"

Warmth and happiness fill my chest. While my wings keep up their steady beat, I nuzzle my snout into his shoulder. "I forgive you." The barest breeze moves over the crown of my dragon's head as Maxon ruffles my scales.

Some things never change, I guess. I'll always be his little sister. For once, that doesn't seem like such as bad thing. I suppose becoming Empress makes me value the few places in my life where I can still hide in the shadows.

Maxon turns to Tempest. "What d'you say, T? Are we good?"

Tempest winks. "We're good."

Maxon's smoky face breaks out into a huge smile. "Since we're late coming to the party, Li and I wanted to do something special. Try and make up for things."

"You don't have to do anything. Just being here is enough."

"Nah, I'm the Monarrki of Air. I can do more than show up." He turns to Lianna, who's drifted over to his side. "Ready?"

Lianna rubs her hands together. "You know it."

Maxon raises his left hand. A thin column of wind cuts through the clouds over our heads. A beam of bright light pokes through. Lianna raises her hand as well, adding a swirl of raindrops into the new brightness.

I gasp when I see the results. Rainbows appear everywhere. And I thought the angelic choir was going to break me. Rainbows from my gruff brother kick the angelic choir in the gut and call it names. Philosophically speaking, of course.

"That's beautiful, Maxon."

"You like it?"

"Yes." My voice breaks. "I don't know what to say."

"It's the first of its kind, anywhere," says Lianna proudly.

My lower lip trembles. "Thank you."

"You still all right, luv?"

My eyes line with warm tears. Suddenly, it seems like a huge miss that dragons don't have pockets or extraordinarily large handkerchiefs for situations like this. "Yes, I think so."

"Are those happy tears?"

The choir hits a crescendo. My chest feels so full of joy, it could burst. "Definitely." I clear my throat. "I'm ready to declare the end to this Procession now."

Tempest beams. "Ace it again."

I inhale a deep breath and try my best to pull myself together. Although now, the Furor nation is so overjoyed with the free angelic concert and rainbow light show, I think I could burst into flame and they wouldn't care. I cast another quick spell to enhance my voice.

"My people!" I cry.

They keep cavorting through the skies and darting in between rainbows.

Tempest's irises turn demon-bright. A low growl echoes from his chest. Everyone quiets, even the angelic choir. Tempest's been teaching me all sorts of dragon stuff lately. That's another trick I'll have to add to the list.

"My people," I continue. "You've touched my heart with your warm welcome. I can't wait to lead with Tempest at my side. I hereby declare this Procession complete!"

The Furor all roar together. The sound is deafening and beautiful.

I close my eyes. A memory appears. I'm running down the marble staircase of the Ryder Mansion, worried about being late for my lecture. Back then, my life then was magic, Firmament, and family. The closest I'd had to a boyfriend was that drycleaner guy.

I shake my head in amazement.

As of today, my magic has changed from almost impossible to nearly all-powerful. My family includes a nation of dragons. And my love life? That's the best change of all. I nuzzle into Tempest's neck. His dragon scales feel warm and leathery. "The Procession's over. Let's go home."

Tempest gently links his front claw with mine. My chest fills with warmth and love. "There, now," says Tempest. "I'm home already."

I remember the first time I saw him on that balcony, a few months and a thousand years ago. Part of me knew it then, too. Wherever Tempest is, that's my heart's home. Together, we fly off into the clouds.

The End

Keep an eye out for *Cursed*, the first book in the new Beholder series from Christina Bauer. For more information, go to:
www.inkmonster.net

BECOMING
ALPHA
AILEEN ERIN

THE SHADOW
RAVENS
CIPHER
AILEEN ERIN

Acknowledgements

You. Me. We.

That was my mantra when I was writing the *Angelbound* books. It all started when I got on this kick about team-style relationships where the 'you' and 'me' create something different. The 'we.' I started thinking about it a ton, and then my Little Nagging Voice got into the act.

"Hey," said LNV. "What if we wrote books where the relationship conflict isn't based on anyone having misunderstandings and such? Genuine partnerships only. We could come up with cool ways for them to team, like with battle moves."

I decided that the LNV was onto something. The game was afoot.

In the first three *Angelbound* books—*Angelbound, Scala, Armageddon*—the hero and heroine fight as a team. No one fights the baddie solo. In Book 4, *Maxon,* I took a break and went back to a more traditional rescue set-up. That said, the big magilla was always, always *Portia*. I have been jonesing to use magic as a metaphor for two people coming together for ages. I hadn't found any authors in my space who'd done that yet (not that they aren't out there!) I'm an entrepreneur, and I love building stuff. I was so freaking excited, I couldn't stand my bad self.

On a side note, there was another reason I did this. The stories we tell are important and I am a big fan of teamwork. Now, some of you may think I went too far in this story. Others, not far enough. All I can say is that I did my best to fight the good fight. Nuff said.

So, if I did my job right, you should have been caught up in the story and never noticed any of this new paradigm gobbledygook. But since this is the acknowledgments, I can speak my mind and say that *Portia* kicked my ass and called me a bitch. In bringing her story to life, I have strained every major relationship I have. All of which is a long way of saying that I have a lot of people to thank this time around. Buckle up, friends!

To begin with, I would like to thank my day job, aka the lovely people at software developer Zerto. My team's unwavering interest and support mean a lot. Thank you, Mariah West, Christina Saint-Pierre, and Gil Levonai!

Next, I must suck up to the amazing folks at INscribe Digital, who move mountains and make it look easy. Kelly Peterson, Guillian Heltzer, Stephanie Gomes, Allison Davis, and Anne Kubek. You amaze me.

Time for the Ink Monsters! Candace, you got

thrown in the deep end and didn't give up. You're my hero! And Aileen? No one edits like you, girlfriend. You're a freaking prodigy. Now Lola, my dear Lola! I think the only person who slept less than me would be YOU! And yet your whip-fast mind always found ways to make things better. What a joy you are.

Can't forget Kim Stern! You introduced me to Aileen and got the Ink Monster ball rolling. More important, you were a true friend to Matt, Max, and me when we needed it most. Love in AEO.

Best for last. Huge and heartfelt thanks to my husband and son. You supported me through everything from long nights to taping balloons all over the living room so I can block out a scene. None of this would be possible without you. Je t'aime.

And no list is truly complete until I thank whatever reader liked this book enough to actually finish the Acknowledgements. Hey you, awesome reader! You're amazing. Thanks! Now like me on Facebook and we can send snarky messages to each other. Huzzah!

Christina Bauer graduated from Syracuse University's Newhouse School with BA's in English along with Television, Radio, and Film Production. An avowed girl geek, Christina loves creating immersive fantasy worlds with action, adventure, romance, and kick-ass female protagonists. As part of her work in Ink Monster, Christina has co-developed the 'Heroine's Journey,' a blueprint for telling female myths inspired by the work of Joseph Campbell. She lives in Newton, MA with her husband, son, and golden retriever Ruby.

Printed in Great Britain
by Amazon.co.uk, Ltd.,
Marston Gate.